If I Had One Wish...

OTHER YEARLING BOOKS YOU WILL ENJOY:

THE CASE OF THE DIRTY BIRD, *Gary Paulsen*
DUNC'S DOLL, *Gary Paulsen*
CULPEPPER'S CANNON, *Gary Paulsen*
DUNC GETS TWEAKED, *Gary Paulsen*
BABE RUTH AND THE HOME RUN DERBY, *Stephen Mooser*
THE TERRIBLE TICKLER, *Stephen Mooser*
NEKOMAH CREEK, *Linda Crew*
SHILOH, *Phyllis Reynolds Naylor*
SOUP IN LOVE, *Robert Newton Peck*
SOUP'S UNCLE, *Robert Newton Peck*

YEARLING BOOKS/YOUNG YEARLINGS/YEARLING CLASSICS are designed especially to entertain and enlighten young people. Patricia Reilly Giff, consultant to this series, received her bachelor's degree from Marymount College and a master's degree in history from St. John's University. She holds a Professional Diploma in Reading and a Doctorate of Humane Letters from Hofstra University. She was a teacher and reading consultant for many years, and is the author of numerous books for young readers.

For a complete listing of all Yearling titles,
write to Dell Readers Service,
P.O. Box 1045,
South Holland, IL 60473.

If I Had One Wish...

by

Jackie French Koller

A Yearling Book

Published by
Dell Publishing
a division of
Bantam Doubleday Dell Publishing Group, Inc.
1540 Broadway
New York, New York 10036

The characters and events in this book are fictitious. Any similarity to real persons, living or dead, is coincidental and not intended by the author.

The trademark Yearling® is registered in the U.S. Patent and Trademark Office.

The trademark Dell® is registered in the U.S. Patent and Trademark Office.

ISBN: 0-440-40807-5

Reprinted by arrangement with Little, Brown and Company (Inc.)

Printed in the United States of America

June 1993

10 9 8 7 6 5 4 3 2 1

OPM

To Ryan, a wish come true . . .

If I Had One Wish...

CHAPTER 1

"Alec? Alec, time to get up. Alec, do you hear me?"

Alec Lansing struggled to open his eyes. He rolled over and tried to focus on the slats of the bunk above him.

"Alec!"

"Yeah, yeah. I hear you, Ma."

"Are you up?"

"Yeah, I'm up."

The world outside Alec's window was still black, and the air in his room was chilled. Alec groaned and tried to work up the courage to throw his covers off and step out onto the cold floor. It seemed an insurmountable task. He looked over at the lighted numbers on his clock. 6:10. What could another five minutes hurt? He closed his eyes and rolled over, curling deliciously into the snug folds of his blanket. A warm, blissful fuzziness invaded his mind once again.

"Alec!"

Alec shot bolt upright in the bed and stared at the clock. 6:30! "Oh, shoot," he mumbled. He'd done it again.

"Alec! What am I going to do with you? You said you were up. If you miss that bus . . . "

Alec hopped out of bed, banging his head on the top bunk in his haste. A string of profanities raced through his mind, but he knew better than to say any of them out loud. "Shoot!" he repeated instead.

"Alec!"

"I'm up, I'm up! I'll make it, Ma. Don't worry." He wrapped his quilt around himself, grabbed some clean underwear, and staggered down the hall to the bathroom. He opened the medicine cabinet and took out his toothbrush.

"Make it quick, Alec," his father yelled from his own bathroom on the other side of the medicine cabinet.

"Yeah, yeah."

Alec stepped into the shower and turned on the faucets.

"Agh!" he shrieked as a frigid blast hit him in the face. His older sister had left the control on *shower* rather than *tub* again. Alec had to reach back through the icy curtain of spray and turn up the hot water. "I'm gonna kill you when I get out, Kelly!" he shouted, even though he knew she was probably downstairs at breakfast already. Kelly, the perfect one, never overslept.

Alec adjusted the water to warm, leaned into it, and closed his eyes again. After what seemed like two seconds, he heard the usual loud banging on the bathroom wall.

"Yeah, yeah," he mumbled, switching off the water and stepping out onto the bath mat. He pulled the vanity door open and groped underneath for a towel. "Shoot." Perfect One had cleaned them out again. Alec would never understand how she could use five towels at a time. He banged on the bathroom wall.

"Dad?"

"Yeah?"

"Got any towels over there?"

"Yeah. Hold on."

Alec stood, cold, wet, and miserable, trying to rub the goose bumps off his arms.

"Dad?"

"I'm coming. Hold on."

His father finally pushed the door open a crack and shoved a towel through. It was already damp.

"Aren't there any clean ones?"

"There's nothing wrong with that one. It's barely used."

Alec sighed, rubbed himself down with the damp towel, and slipped on his undershorts. He dried his hair with one quick stroke and pulled his undershirt over his head. He leaned in close and examined his face in the mirror. No new zits. That was good. But no new hair either. He took a couple of swipes at his cheeks with his sister's razor anyway, just in case.

"Alec," yelled his father, "you don't have time to admire yourself. Let's go."

Alec frowned. Sometimes he swore his parents had hidden cameras all over the house. He put on the rest of his clothes and went down for breakfast, taking a moment to sneak into the living room for a quick sniff of the Christmas tree. He breathed deeply of the fresh, woodsy scent. "*Ahhh . . .*"

"Alec!"

"Coming . . ." Alec dashed down the hall, jumping up and banging his head into the little snowman chime that hung in the doorway. The cheerful jingle announced his arrival in the kitchen. His father and Kelly looked up. Their breakfast plates were nearly empty already.

"It's about time," his father grumbled. "Sit down and eat. You've got five minutes."

Alec looked at the clock. He actually had fifteen minutes, but his father made a hobby out of rushing people.

Alec's mother looked up from her coffee and smiled, but then her smiled faded. "Alec," she said, "those pants look like you slept in them."

Alec slid into his chair. "They're fine, Ma."

"They are not fine," Alec's mother went on. "I hate you to look all rumpled like that. Wherever did you find them?"

"They're fine," Alec repeated. "They were in my closet."

Kelly snorted. "Yeah, right," she said, "your under-the-bed closet."

"Oh, thank you, Perfect One," said Alec, bowing his head three times in Kelly's direction. "Thank you for pointing out yet another of my hideous flaws. I will strive to do better, I promise."

Kelly grimaced. "Grow up, Alec, will you?" she said.

"Grow up? If you so command, O Perfect One."

"All right, never mind," said Alec's mother. "Let's call a truce and get on with breakfast, okay?"

Alec poured himself a heaping bowl of cornflakes. He added milk, and the cornflakes rose up and fell over the edges of the bowl onto the table. He scooped them into his hand and shoved them into his mouth before anyone noticed.

"We're getting our report cards today," Kelly announced cheerfully.

Alec grimaced. "Thanks for sharing that," he said.

Alec's father turned to him. "Don't the high school and the junior high get report cards on the same day?" he asked.

Alec dropped his head and nodded.

"What is your report card going to look like, Alec?" his father asked.

Alec tensed. "I don't know."

"What do you mean, you don't know?"

"I mean I don't know. Why don't you ever ask Kelly what her report card is going to look like?"

His father stared at him gravely. "I don't *have* to ask Kelly what her report card is going to look like."

Out of the corner of his eye Alec could see Kelly grinning smugly. He felt the muscles of his jaw tighten.

"I'm waiting for an answer, Alec," his father persisted.

"It'll be fine, Dad," he mumbled.

"Pardon?"

"It'll be *fine,* Dad!"

Alec's father's eyes flashed fire. "Don't raise your voice to me, Alec!"

"John, please," said Alec's mother. "What's the point of all this? You'll see the report card tonight. Can't we just finish our breakfast in peace?"

Anger boiled in Alec's veins, but he held it in, even though it made him tremble. He'd been through this so many times with his father, and he never got anywhere. It was a battle that couldn't be won. He swallowed his anger like bitter medicine and turned back to his breakfast.

"I just asked him a question, Meg," Alec's father said. "I don't see what he always has to get so defensive about."

They ate in silence for a while. Alec poured himself a second bowl of cereal, then a third.

"Alec," said his mother, laughing a little, "how many bowls are you going to eat?"

Alec's father's mood suddenly shifted, and he smiled widely. "Let him eat," he said, pounding Alec proudly on the back. "He's a growing boy."

The fact that Alec was the tallest boy in the eighth grade, six foot two, seemed to be one of the few things Alec's father liked about him. Unfortunately, being tall wasn't enough by itself.

"Got a game today?" his father asked.

Alec's jaw tightened again. "No."

"Monday?"

Alec nodded.

"Good. You gonna play?"

"I don't know, Dad."

"What do you mean, you don't know?"

The tension started to build again.

"I mean I don't know. The coach didn't tell us yet."

"Well, of course you're gonna play. You're the tallest kid on the basketball team. Why wouldn't you?"

Alec's grip tightened on his spoon. "Because I stink, that's why," he mumbled into his bowl.

"What, Alec?"

"Nothing, Dad."

"Well, of course you're going to play," his father repeated. "You've got to want it, that's all — gotta get that eye of the tiger. Why, when I was your age nothing could stop me from playing. When the going gets tough . . ."

"The tough get going. I know, Dad." Alec nodded. He'd heard it all before. Every soccer season. Every basketball season. Every baseball season. Every dreaded sports season of the year. Sometimes he wished he'd been born a scrawny runt.

"Look at your sister," his dad went on. "She used to be just an average soccer player. But she worked and worked, and look at her now, MVP of the league in her junior year!" He grinned proudly at Kelly.

Alec abruptly pushed his bowl away and stood up.

"Where are you going?" his father asked.

"I gotta get my books."

"But I was talking to you."

● 7

Alec wavered a moment, then sighed and sat back down heavily.

His father stared at him in silence, then shook his head and turned away. "I don't understand him, Meg," he said to Alec's mom in a wounded voice. "All I'm trying to do is help."

Alec's mother looked at them both with mournful eyes. "Alec," she said, "try not to be so short tempered. Dad is just interested in you, that's all."

Alec bit his lip and stared up at the ceiling. So now it was his fault. How did everything always end up his fault?

There was a shuffling step in the hallway, and Stevie appeared in the doorway, rubbing the sleep from his eyes. His parents' spirits seemed to lift instantaneously.

"Hello, Pooh," said his mother warmly, reaching out to Stevie.

"Hi there, little guy," said his father. "Come give Dad a big hug."

Alec watched as his six-year-old brother went from one parent to the other to be smothered with hugs and kisses. He thought back sullenly to the days before Stevie, the days when they had loved *him* like that.

Stevie slid into his place at the table and poured himself a heaping bowl of Crunchy Bears. He added milk, and the Crunchy Bears rose up and fell over the edges of the bowl into the table.

Alec scowled at him. "Watch what you're doing, you little slob," he said.

CHAPTER 2

It had been snowing lightly all day, unusual for mid-December in Meadowbrook, Massachusetts, and Alec found it hard to keep his mind on his work. All he could think about were the new skis he'd gotten for his thirteenth birthday, and the chance that he might get to try them out tomorrow.

Report cards were handed out at the end of last period. Alec shoved his quickly into his notebook and filed out the door. He'd look at it later, when none of his friends were around. Mrs. McGarry, his English teacher, waved to him from across the hall.

"Alec," she called, "can I speak to you a minute?"

Alec walked over, and they stepped inside her door.

"I just wanted to explain something to you before you look at your report card," said Mrs. McGarry.

Alec was puzzled by her grave expression. What could be wrong? he wondered. English was his best subject.

"I didn't give you the A."

Alec's heart sank. He needed that A to balance C — he knew he was getting in math.

"But why?" he asked. "I had an A average."

"Effort," said Mrs. McGarry quietly. "You're one of the best writers I have, but you could be a lot better. You're just not trying, Alec. We've talked about this before."

Alec stared down at the floor and scuffed at the tile with the toe of his sneaker. "That stinks," he mumbled.

Mrs. McGarry touched Alec's shoulder, and when he looked up at her again, she was smiling kindly. "I know you think I'm being mean," she said, "but someday you'll understand. You've got a special talent, and I just want you to learn to make the most of it, okay?"

Alec shrugged and nodded, mainly because he figured that's what Mrs. McGarry expected. What did writing have to do with life anyway?

"Good," said Mrs. McGarry. She gave his arm a squeeze. "Now you have a great weekend and come back on Monday ready to work for that A."

Alec managed a halfhearted smile, then shuffled back out into the hall. Have a great weekend? Obviously Mrs. McGarry didn't know his father. How did he always end up in this predicament? He started every semester determined to work hard, but somehow there always seemed to be so many more exciting things to do than study.

"*Hey, Giraffeman!*"

Alec turned around. Muzzy Franklin, his best friend, was bobbing toward him through the crowd, his baseball cap disappearing and then reappearing again, like a buoy riding on a rough sea.

"How'd you do?" Muzzy asked when he finally broke through. He was waving his own report card in the air.

Alec smiled down at him. "I don't know," he said, "but you look happy enough. You must've done okay."

Muzzy shrugged. "Not too shabby. Three A's and the rest B's."

Alec nodded. He'd expected as much. Muzzy was just as much a brain as Kelly, and just as strong an athlete, too, but somehow it was easier to take perfection in a best friend than in an older sister.

"Doing anything after school?" Alec asked.

"I don't know. Got a hockey game but that's not till seven-thirty."

"Wanna do something?"

"I thought you had practice, man."

"I'm not going."

"Why not?"

"I hurt my knee in gym."

Muzzy looked skeptical. "You're not limping," he said.

Alec frowned. "It *hurts,* Muzzer," he repeated.

"You tell Costanzo yet?"

"Yeah."

"What'd he say?"

"Not much."

Muzzy raised an eyebrow. "He won't put you in the game Monday."

"Good," said Alec with a wry smile. "Then nobody will see how bad I stink."

"Good attitude, Giraffeman. Why'd you even go out for the team if you hate it so bad?"

"You know why."

Muzzy shook his head. "I wouldn't play hockey if I didn't like it. I wouldn't care what my old man wanted."

Alec gave him a wry smile. "Wanna bet?" he said. Muzzy's dad had been a star athlete when he was a kid, just like Alec's father. And like Kelly, Muzzy's older brother had followed right in his father's footsteps. The only difference was, Muzzy had inherited the family prowess, too.

Muzzy grinned. "Yeah, I guess maybe I would," he said.

Alec laughed. "You *know* you would."

They pushed their way through the front doors of the school.

"*Hey, Giraffe!*"

Alec turned, and a snowball hit him square in the mouth. Mike Finkelstein burst out laughing. "Sorry, Alec," he yelled. "You just make such a great target."

Alec dropped his books and scooped up a mound of snow. "You better run, *Frankenstein*," he yelled. The next thing he knew, snowballs were whizzing every which way. Girls were shrieking, and guys were laughing. It was the best fun Alec had had in days. He packed a great big one and aimed it at Mike.

"*Lansing!*"

The vice-principal's voice boomed out over the crowd. Alec looked at him.

"Drop that snowball and get on your bus!"

Alec dropped his snowball and looked down at Muzzy.

"What?" he whispered. "Am I the only one throwing snowballs?"

Muzzy chuckled. "Naw," he answered. "You're just the easiest one to see."

CHAPTER 3

The house smelled sweet and spicy when Alec walked in the door. Fresh-baked pieces of gingerbread were stacked up on the kitchen counter, waiting for the family to assemble them that evening into the traditional gingerbread house. Alec's mother was just finishing washing up the pans.

"Alec?" she said, looking up in surprise. "What are you doing home so soon?"

"No practice today." said Alec. It was easier than explaining the truth. He grabbed a little piece of gingerbread.

"Hey," said his mother, playfully slapping his hand, "put that down. That's a door."

Alec frowned. "Well, aren't there any scraps?"

"Aren't there always?" his mom answered with a smile. She pulled the bread box open to reveal a plateful of odd-shaped pieces.

Alec scooped up a handful and shoved them into his mouth. "Mmmm," he mumbled, "good."

Alec's mother went back to drying the pans. "No practice?" she said. "Isn't that strange, with a game on Monday?"

"Yeah. I guess the coach is sick or something."

"Oh . . . ?" said his mother. "Well, that's great."

Alec looked at her.

"I mean, it's not great that the coach is sick. It's great that you're home. Now I won't have to pay a sitter for Stevie."

"Aw, Ma. Where's Kelly?"

"She's got an indoor soccer match today, and I've got a class."

"Aw, c'mon, Ma. I'll pay the sitter out of my birthday money."

"Alec, don't be foolish. That would be throwing money away, especially when there's no reason why you can't watch your brother."

"Yes there is. He's a pest."

Alec's mother smiled and winked at him. "You were a pest when you were six years old, too, but we all put up with you."

"I wasn't as much of a pest as he is."

"Wanna bet?"

The phone rang and Alec dived on it. "It's for me," he said.

"What else is new?" His mom chuckled.

It was the Muzzer. "Hey, Giraffeman. Cindy and Liz just called. They and a number of other lovelies are going

● 15

out to the mall to do some Christmas shopping, and they would like us to get the main men together and meet them there."

Muzzy's colorful way of putting things made Alec smile. "That sounds great," he said. "Hold on."

His mother had just stepped into her boots and was pulling on her coat.

"Hey, Ma," said Alec, "Muzzy wants to know if we can go to the mall."

"No," his mother stated emphatically. "I can't drive or pick up, and —"

"No sweat," Muzzy shouted through the phone. "We have a ride both ways."

"We have a ride both ways," Alec repeated. "Come on, Ma, please?"

"No, Alec. You know I don't like you hanging around the mall, and besides, you have to watch Stevie."

"We're not hanging around. We're Christmas shopping."

"Alec, I don't have time to argue. You're watching Stevie."

Alec's shoulders sagged. He pressed the phone against his ear again. "I can't," he said despondently. "I gotta watch Stevie."

"So?" said Muzzy. "Bring the brat along."

"Really?"

"Why not?"

Alec's mother was on her way out.

"Ma, wait!"

"What is it now, Alec?"

"How about if we take Stevie along?"

There was a silence, which Alec took as an encouraging sign. At least she was considering it.

"I don't know, Alec. I worry about you kids out at that mall."

"Aw, c'mon, Ma. You worry too much. We'll be fine. And Stevie'll love it. You know how he always wants to do everything I do."

Another silence.

"I'll watch him like a hawk, Ma. I promise. And we'll be back by six sharp, and . . . I'll make dinner!"

Alec's mother arched an eyebrow. "*You'll* make dinner?"

"Sure," said Alec. "I can do it. Kelly does it all the time. You'll see. Please let us go . . ."

"Oh, all right." Alec's mother sounded more worn down than convinced. "But if anything happens to that little boy, Alec . . ."

"Nothing's gonna happen, Ma. I promise. He'll have a ball."

Alec's mother left for her law school class, and a short time later Stevie came trudging slowly up the driveway, trying to catch snowflakes on his tongue.

"Hurry up, butt head," Alec yelled to him from the door. "Muzzy's mom is gonna be here any minute to pick us up."

"Pick who up?" asked Stevie.

"You and me," said Alec. "We're going to the mall."

Stevie's face fell. "I don't wanna go to the mall," he protested. "I wanna go sledding."

"You can go sledding tomorrow. Right now you're going to the mall."

"But I don't wanna go to the mall," Stevie started whining.

"Don't whine," said Alec. "I hate it when you whine."

"I'm not whining," Stevie whined.

"Just get in here and get your snack and go to the bathroom and do whatever it is you do when you get home from school. Muzzy's mother is on the way, and you're going to the mall whether you want to or not."

Stevie's eyes filled with tears, and he trudged past Alec. "It's not fair," he mumbled. "All day in school I couldn't wait to get home and go sledding."

Alec remembered his own skiing daydreams and felt a stab of guilt.

"Tell you what," he said. "I'll give you a couple of bucks and you can go into Toy Town and get yourself one of your dumb Rat Pack guys."

Stevie's eyes lit up. "Really?"

"I just said I would, didn't I?"

"Neat-o!"

Muzzy's mother's van pulled into the driveway.

"Here she is," said Alec. "Let's go."

"But I didn't have my snack."

"I'll get you something there."

"But I —"

"Never mind. Just *move it,* you little creep." Alec gave Stevie a push out the door.

There were six guys crowded into the van already. Alec

made Stevie sit up front with Mrs. Franklin, and he squeezed into the middle seat next to Muzzy.

"I don't know, Alec," joked Mrs. Franklin. "You grow any taller and we'll have to trade this van in for one of those high-top jobs."

Alec smiled and wished he could think of something funny to say in return, but somehow his quick wit always deserted him around adults. Mrs. Franklin didn't seem to expect an answer anyway. She turned on the radio and started humming to herself.

"I got bad news, man," Muzzy whispered.

Alec looked at him. "About what?"

"Cindy."

"What about her?"

"She's gonna dump you."

"When?"

"Today."

"Why?"

"She wants to go out with Frankenstein."

Alec turned to look at Mike, who shrugged and turned his hands palms upward in a gesture of innocence.

"I didn't ask her," he said. "Honest, I didn't know anything about it."

Alec frowned and shook his head. He didn't feel any great affection for Cindy, but he liked going out with her because she was the most popular girl in school. He'd always known it wouldn't last, though. Cindy seemed determined to go out with every good-looking guy in school before the year was out.

"So what?" he said. "I was gonna dump her anyway."

CHAPTER 4

The mall was festively trimmed and crowded with shoppers. Christmas carols blared over the loudspeaker.

"Can we go to Toy Town now?" asked Stevie as soon as they arrived.

"In a minute," said Alec. Then he turned to Muzzy. "Where did they say they'd be?"

"Forgot to ask," said Muzzy. "Let's try the food court."

"Can I have my snack now?" asked Stevie.

"In a minute," said Alec. They walked from one end of the food court to the other, but the girls weren't anywhere in sight.

"Let's try the pet shop," Mike suggested. "They always go to look at the puppies."

"What about my snack?" asked Stevie.

"I told you, we'll get it in a minute," said Alec.

"I have to go to the bathroom," said Stevie.

Alec rolled his eyes. "All right, go ahead. We'll wait right here."

"Mommy says I'm not allowed to go alone," said Stevie.

Alec sighed. "I'll be right back," he told the guys. Then he grabbed Stevie by the collar. "C'mon, butt head," he grumbled.

When they got back from the men's room, the girls had arrived. Alec approached Cindy hesitantly, wondering if she was going to dump him publicly in front of the whole mall. She smiled at him warmly.

"Hi Alec," she said, reaching out to take his hand. Alec looked over at Muzzy, who shrugged as if to say, "Maybe I got the story wrong."

Alec smiled. It wouldn't be the first time. He took Cindy's hand in his.

"Can I have my snack *now?*" asked Stevie.

"In a minute," said Alec.

"You keep saying that," said Stevie, "and I'm starting to get a headache."

Cindy smiled and brushed Stevie's sandy hair out of his eyes. "Oh, Alec," she said, "go get your little brother an ice cream cone."

Alec frowned. "All right," he said. "I'll be right back."

"And get me one, too," Cindy called after him.

"What kind?"

"Death by Chocolate."

The ice cream bar was way over at the opposite end of the food court. Alec walked past all the other fast food booths, took a number, and got into a line about twenty people deep. By the time he got back with the two ice cream cones, the girls were gone and the guys were all standing around looking miffed.

"Where'd they go?" asked Alec.

"They left," said Mike.

"What do you mean, 'left'?"

"The *mouth* here" — Muzzy jerked his thumb at Stevie — "told your lady you were gonna dump her."

"He what?!" Alec looked down at Stevie, who squirmed under his gaze.

"Well you said you were," he whined. "I heard you in the car."

Alec was starting to burn. "You weren't supposed to be listening to that, you little eavesdropper," he said, "and even if I did say it, what business did you have telling her?"

"I was helping you," Stevie said. "I wanted to tell her before she told you."

"I don't need your help, you little nerd," Alec roared. "Just stay out of my life!"

Stevie's bottom lip quivered.

"Ah, take it easy on him," said Mike. "He's just a dumb little kid. He thought he was doing you a favor."

"He's a dumb little butt head," Alec corrected him. The ice cream cones were starting to drip over his hands. "Here," he said, shoving one of them at Stevie, "plug your mouth up for a while, will you?"

Alec licked the other one. "Yuck," he said. "I hate Death by Chocolate."

"I'll gladly take it off your hands," offered Muzzy.

"You wanna pay me the two bucks I just spent for it?" asked Alec.

"Well, I'm not sure I want it *that* bad."

"Oh, here," said Alec. He handed Muzzy the cone and sat down heavily in the booth across from Stevie. What else could go wrong today?

"Can I play a video game now?" Stevie asked hesitantly.

"Not on your life," said Alec.

"Then can we go get my toy now?"

Alec shot him a look fit to kill. "What are you, stupid?" he said. "You can forget the toy."

Stevie's mouth dropped open. "But you promised," he cried.

"Well, I'm breaking my promise."

Tears filled Stevie's eyes. "You promised, you promised," he started to whine. "I'm gonna tell Mommy you broke your promise."

Tears streamed down his cheeks, and his nose started running, and then the ice cream cone began to drip all over his new green ski coat.

"Oh, all right. Just shut up," said Alec. Then he turned to Muzzy. "I'm gonna kill him," he said, "and you, too. *Bring him along.* Great idea, butt head senior."

Muzzy grinned. "You have a very limited vocabulary, you know that, Giraffeman?" He grabbed a bunch of napkins and started cleaning Stevie up. "Look," he went on, "let's go get the kid his toy so he'll shut up. Then we can try to find the ladies and explain."

"Explain what?"

"I don't know, man. We'll think of something."

CHAPTER 5

Toy Town had a whole aisle full of Rat Pack guys hanging on hooks ten deep, and Stevie had to look at every last one of them before he made his decision. Alec was getting angrier and angrier, and the rest of the gang was losing patience.

"Here," Alec said, thrusting one of the guys into Stevie's hand, "what's wrong with this one?"

"He's a good guy, and I already have enough good guys. I need more bad guys."

"Okay, then how about this one?" He picked up some kind of a green swamp-monster figure.

"No, he's the slime-mobile driver, and I don't have a slime-mobile."

Alec rolled his eyes.

Muzzy looked at his watch. "My mom's gonna be back in half an hour," he said.

"All right, that does it," Alec said to Stevie. "Pick one right now or we're leaving with nothing."

Stevie glared at him, but he finally grabbed a package and marched over to the register.

"Look," said Mike when they got back out into the mall, "there go the girls!"

Alec whirled around. "Where?"

Mike pointed. "Down there, on the lower level."

They all started toward the stairs, but then Alec stopped. "Wait a minute, guys," he said. "What about big ears here?" He nodded at Stevie.

"Give the boy a couple of quarters and let him go to the arcade," suggested Muzzy.

"Yeah!" shouted Stevie.

Alec wavered. He knew his mother wouldn't approve.

Muzzy pointed toward the girls. "C'mon, man. We're gonna lose them again."

"All right, all right." Alec dug into his pocket and pulled out a handful of quarters. "Go straight to the arcade," he told Stevie, "and stay there. I'll be back in five minutes."

Stevie grabbed the quarters and took off.

"*C'mon,* Giraffeman," yelled Muzzy. "They disappeared again."

The whole gang of boys charged down the curved staircase, with Alec a few steps behind. There was an old woman making her way laboriously up the stairs. Mike banged into her in his haste. She grabbed the railing to stop herself from falling, but Mike's body nearly wrenched the shopping bag from her other hand. It tore open, spilling its contents all down the stairs. Mike and the others kept right on going without a backward glance. Alec ran by a few steps, too, but then he turned and looked back. The old woman was clutching her chest. She seemed to be having trouble breathing.

"Alec, come on," Mike shouted. "Hurry up."

Alec looked after his friends. They were rapidly disappearing into the crowd in search of the girls, but somehow he couldn't bring himself to follow. He turned and climbed back up to the old woman.

"Are you okay?" he asked.

She looked up at him with frightened eyes. Her face was deeply lined and leathery. She was dressed in layers of soiled old clothing that smelled of perspiration. A faded scarf of once-bright colors was knotted under her chin, and a few wisps of straight gray hair escaped from it here and there. She started to cough, a deep, wracking cough.

"Are you okay?" Alec asked again. He began to wonder if she understood English, but at last she caught her breath and nodded.

"I'm sorry about my friends," said Alec. "They didn't mean anything. They were just in a hurry. I'm sure they didn't realize . . ."

The woman said nothing. Her breathing slowed, and she bent to retrieve her things. Her legs were thick and purple, and bending seemed to be a tremendous effort for her. She began to cough again.

"Here, let me do that for you," said Alec.

He started picking things up off the stairs. There was

a strange assortment: empty cans, a box of dry cat food, pieces of clothing, safety pins, a wad of brown paper towels, a ball of string, some tin foil. . . . Alec went to put everything back into the bag, but the side was ripped all the way down. He looked around. At the bottom of the stairs was a gourmet food shop with a shopping bag dispenser just inside the door. Alec piled the woman's belongings on the step by her feet.

"Wait right here," he said. "I'm just going to run down and get you another bag."

The woman stared at him blankly, giving no indication of whether she'd understood.

Alec touched her arm gently. "Just wait here," he said, "I'll be right back."

He hopped down the stairs and hurried over to the food shop. He looked over his shoulder. The woman was still there. "Wait," he mouthed to her again, holding up a finger to indicate that he'd only be a minute. He dropped a coin into the slot and took a bag out of the dispenser, then dashed back up the stairs. He carefully placed the woman's belongings into the bag, then folded up her old bag and tucked that in as well. He handed her the new bag.

She took it and nodded shortly. Then she turned and started up the stairs again. She lifted one leg, then the other, slowly and wearily. Her hand trembled as she slid it along the railing.

Alec stepped up beside her and reached for the bag.

"Here," he said, "let me take that for you." She gave him a slightly mistrustful glance, but she allowed him to take the bag. He slid his free hand under her elbow. "Come on," he said. "I'll help you up the stairs." She glanced at him briefly again, but then nodded and leaned into his arm as she began to climb.

The woman was heavy, and progress was slow. Alec was sweating inside his ski jacket before they'd gone more than a few steps, and it was all he could do to keep from holding his nose. The woman's breathing was raspy and loud. She coughed intermittently. Alec looked at her with concern.

"You know," he told her, "you should take the escalator. They have one at each end of the mall."

"Humph," said the old woman.

Alec smiled. So she did understand English. "Yeah, I know," he told her. "I used to be scared of them, too. I used to be afraid my foot would get caught and I'd get dragged down inside the machinery."

The woman stopped and looked at him. Her eyes were a surprisingly lively blue. She seemed to search his face for a moment. Then she moved on again.

"There's an elevator in Sears," Alec went on. "You could try that next time."

"Humph," said the woman again.

Alec shrugged. "Don't like elevators either, huh?"

The woman didn't answer.

When they reached the top, Alec steered the woman to one side and waited with her a moment until she got through another coughing spell. At last she reached for the bag.

"You're sure you're all right?" said Alec.

The woman nodded.

"You want me to walk you to the door or anything?"

She shook her head.

"Okay," said Alec. "I'm sorry, again, about my friends."

He started to turn away, when he felt a hand on his arm.

He turned back. The old woman was staring up at him again. She squeezed his arm. "You are a good boy," she said. Her voice was strangely youthful and melodious.

Alec blushed and tried to gently pull away, but the woman wouldn't loosen her grasp. She put her bag down on the floor and reached into her pocket. She leaned against him secretively and tried to press a coin into his hand. Alec pushed it back.

"No, no" he said. "I don't want any money."

The woman pressed more firmly. "It's not money," she said softly.

Alec looked down at the coin in his hand. It looked like one of the game tokens from Fun World, but it had some kind of strange squiggles on it.

"It is a talisman," said the old woman.

"A talisman?" Alec repeated.

The old woman nodded gravely. "It will give you one wish," she whispered. "Use it with care."

Alec stared into the woman's small, bright eyes, shining with sincerity. Obviously she was crazy as a coot, but if it gave her pleasure to give him her gumball-machine trinket, he might as well play along.

"Thank you," he said, trying to hide a smile. "That's very kind of you."

She squeezed his hand once more before she let him go. "Use it with care," she warned again. Then she hobbled away.

Alec shoved the coin into his jeans pocket and stood staring after her, wondering who she was and where she would go.

"That was nice."

The voice interrupted Alec's thoughts and he turned to see who it belonged to. The voice's owner was a beautiful girl with long, golden hair, high cheekbones, and huge, almond-shaped eyes that matched the color of her hair. Alec knew he had seen her before, but he couldn't remember where.

"You're Alec Lansing, aren't you?" she said.

Alec nodded.

"I know your sister, Kelly."

Then Alec remembered. "Oh, yeah," he said. "You're on her softball team, aren't you?"

The girl nodded. "I'm Abbey Bennett," she said.

"Hi Abbey," said Alec, smiling shyly. "Nice to meet you."

"I saw what you did for that woman," Abbey said. "That was really nice."

Alec gave an embarrassed shrug. "It wasn't anything special," he said. "It's what anybody would have done."

Abbey shook her head. "No," she corrected him, "it's what anybody *should've* done, but most people would've kept right on going, like your friends. I know. I see these people ignored all the time."

"*Hey, Giraffeman! We found the ladies. Where've you been?*"

Alec looked back down the stairs. The guys were there and the girls were with them. When Muzzy saw Abbey his mouth fell open, then a slow smile curled his lips. Cindy shot Alec a stormy glance and crossed her arms over her chest.

Abbey smiled. "I guess I better be going," she said, "I don't want to cause you any trouble. Besides, I want to see if that woman needs a lift somewhere. She doesn't look well."

Alec looked back at the old lady. She was still hobbling slowly toward the door.

"That would be nice," he said. Then they both laughed awkwardly.

Abbey put out her hand. "It was *nice* meeting you, Alec Lansing," she said. "I'll look for you next spring at the softball games."

"Yeah," said Alec. He took her hand, and his mouth suddenly went dry.

She pulled her hand slowly away. "Bye, Alec."

"Bye."

He watched her until she caught up with the old lady.

"*Whoa* . . . , who's the fly girl?"

Muzzy had come up the stairs and was standing beside Alec. Alec felt his ears start to burn.

"No one," he said. "She's a friend of Kelly's."

Muzzy gave him a devilish grin.

"Yeah," he said. "She looked *real* friendly."

Alec gave him an elbow in the ribs.

"Don't be stupid, Franklin. She's a junior."

"Didn't seem to bother her none," said Muzzy.

Alec gave him an annoyed grimace and looked over his shoulder down the stairs. "Where'd everybody go?" he asked.

Muzzy shrugged. "Frankenstein and the guys went to buy that new Screaming Trees tape, and the ladies got mad and left again."

"*Again?*" said Alec. "What are they mad about now?"

"Your new *friend*," said Muzzy with an exaggerated wink.

Alec rolled his eyes. "Well, did you at least explain about Stevie?"

"Yeah, don't worry. We got everything straightened out. They were all set to go skiing with us tomorrow, till we caught you with your *friend* there. What were you up to, anyway?"

Alec shook his head. "Nothing. I wasn't with her. I was helping some old lady the whole time."

"Oh, yeah, right," said Muzzy with a laugh. "You're gonna have to do better than that if you're going to convince the ladies, Giraffeman. I don't even buy that one."

"Well, it's true," said Alec, "whether you buy it or not. Let's go find the girls."

"No time," said Muzzy, holding up his watch arm. "We have to get Frankenstein and the rest of the guys and be out in front of Sears in five minutes."

Alec sighed. It was *definitely* not his day.

They rounded up the rest of the guys and arrived at the designated spot just as Mrs. Franklin's van pulled in.

"Great timing, guys" she said. "Did you have fun?"

They all nodded as they climbed aboard. Mrs. Franklin started to pull away, then suddenly stepped on the brake.

"Hold on just a minute," she said. "Aren't we missing somebody?"

They all looked at one another, and suddenly Alec's heart lurched.

"Oh, shoot! Stevie," he said. "I forgot all about Stevie!"

CHAPTER 6

"Promise?" said Alec.

Stevie nodded. "I promise."

Alec handed him the five-dollar bill. "Remember," he cautioned. "You say one word to Mom or Dad about me forgetting you, and I take it back and you won't get to buy that slime-mobile."

"I promise," Stevie reassured him again, bolting out of the kitchen before Alec had a chance to change his mind.

Alec frowned and shook his head. "It's bad enough he ruins my life," he grumbled. "I have to pay him to keep his mouth shut on top of it." Alec looked at the clock. They'd all be home soon, Mom from class first, then Kelly and Dad from the game. He'd better get supper going. He opened the freezer and sorted through the cartons and packages. Corn dogs, he decided, with Dino-fries and baked beans. He pulled out all the necessary packages and turned on the oven, then moved the stacks of gingerbread out of the way. Stevie came out into the kitchen with his drawing paper and crayons. He climbed up on the counter and sat cross-legged, then spread out his papers and began to draw.

"Do you have to do that right here?" Alec growled.

"Uh-huh," said Stevie, tongue clenched pensively between his teeth.

Alec looked up a few minutes later and caught Stevie eyeing him intently.

"What are you staring at?" he snapped.

Stevie shrugged. "Nothin'," he said, bending over his paper again.

Alec scowled. "Don't you have something better to do?"

Stevie shook his head.

Alec rolled his eyes. "Do you *always* have to be wherever I am?"

Stevie looked up and gave him a sheepish grin. "I made you a surprise," he said, handing Alec the piece of paper.

A-L-I-C, it said, in shaky letters across the top. Below was a figure with a head, two long legs, no body, and two short arms sticking sideways out of the head.

"Looks like a clothespin with arms," said Alec, handing it back.

Stevie's smile faded. "I can do a better one," he said, quickly pulling another sheet of paper from the pad.

Alec shook his head. "Look," he said, sliding a stack of dishes out of the cupboard, "quit wasting time. If you really want to surprise me, set the table."

Stevie looked disappointed, but he jumped down and took the heavy stack from Alec. He struggled over without complaint and put the dishes on the table.

"Is that good?" he asked when he had set them all out.

"What are we supposed to eat with, our fingers?" asked Alec.

Stevie opened the silverware drawer and pulled out a handful of utensils. He started placing them on the table.

Alec looked over at him and frowned. "Not those spoons, you wiener," he snapped. "Those are soup spoons."

Stevie flinched, then quickly gathered up the offending spoons and replaced them with correct ones.

"Anything else?" he asked when he'd finished.

"What do you think?" Alec snarled.

Stevie surveyed the table. "Glasses?" he asked.

"Whoa," said Alec, "give the boy a Milkbone."

Stevie giggled. He always laughed at Alec's wry comments, even when they were directed at him.

"Can you reach them for me?" he asked.

"I'm busy," said Alec, pretending to be engrossed in reading the directions on the Dino-fries package.

Stevie climbed back up onto the counter and got to his knees to get the glasses from one of the upper cupboards. One by one he put them on the counter, then climbed down and carried them one by one over to the table.

At last he finished and presented himself in front of Alec once again. "All done," he said, grinning proudly. "Now what?"

"Now get lost," said Alec.

Stevie's grin faded and his small shoulders sagged. He dejectedly pulled his sketchbook and his crayons off the counter and trudged down the hall toward the family room. Alec watched him go, then turned back to the counter. His gaze fell once again on Stevie's childish portrait, and a small pang of guilt tugged at his heart. Maybe he *was* being a little rough on the kid. It wasn't his fault he was such a wiener. . . .

The phone rang and Alec picked it up.

"Hi, Alec." It was Cindy's voice.

"Hi!" said Alec, all concern for Stevie instantaneously forgotten. "I thought you were mad at me."

"Well, I talked to Muzzy and . . ."

There was a sudden rattling in the phone and then the sound of heavy breathing. "Oh, Cindy," Stevie's voice broke in breathlessly. "I love you." He made a series of loud kissy noises, then said, "Will you marry me?" adding more smoochy kisses.

Alec's face started to burn. "Stevie!" he yelled, "get off the extension."

Cindy giggled and the smooching started in again. "Excuse me," Alec yelled into the phone. "I'll call you back later, *after* I murder my little brother!"

CHAPTER 7

Stevie was still hiding in his bedroom when Alec heard the garage door open.

"Hi, boys. I'm home," his mother called. She walked into the kitchen, shaking snow from her scarf. "It's starting to come down heavy out there," she said. "They're talking about eight to twelve inches by morning."

"Great," said Alec. "Can I go skiing with the guys tomorrow?"

"Have you got the money?"

Alec nodded.

"Then I don't see why not." She walked out into the front hall, and Alec heard Stevie bounding down the stairs. He walked innocently into the kitchen, lugging the Christmas Wish Book under his arm, and sat down at the table. He stuck his tongue out at Alec, spread out a bunch of papers, and picked up his pencil.

Alec scowled. "You're not adding to that list again are you?" he asked.

Stevie gave him a sharp glance. "There's only fifteen things on it so far," he said.

"Fifteen!" said Alec. "That's a lot."

"No sir," said Stevie. "Patrick put thirty things on his list last year, and Santa brought them all."

"Oh, yeah, well . . ." With the mood he was in, Alec was tempted to let the cat out of the bag. It was high time somebody told Stevie that there was a limit to what "Santa" could afford, anyway.

"Well, what?" asked Stevie.

"Well . . ." Alec reconsidered. In light of the incident at the mall that afternoon, it probably wasn't a good day to blow Stevie's mind. "Patrick's an only child," he finished.

"So what?"

"So Santa has to split the presents three ways in our house, that's what."

Stevie thought this over a moment, then lowered his pencil and sank down in his chair. "I wish *I* was an only child," he grumbled.

Alec snorted. "You and me both," he said.

Alec's mother came back into the room. "So, Pooh," she said, giving Stevie a hug, "how was your day?"

"Terrible," said Stevie.

Alec could feel his heart speeding up. He gave Stevie a warning glance.

"Terrible?" Alec's mother repeated, kissing Stevie on his chubby cheek. "What could be so terrible?"

"Alec says I can't put as many presents on my list as Patrick because Patrick is an only child and Santa has to split our presents three ways," said Stevie.

Alec let out a silent sigh of relief.

"Is that what Alec said?" Alec's mother shot Alec a quick, reproving glance. "Well, I think you should put whatever you want on your list," she told Stevie, "and let Santa be the judge of what he can and can't bring."

Stevie perked right up. "Really?"

"Really." Alec's mother gave Stevie another hug, and he picked his pencil back up and started delving through the Wish Book again.

Oh sure, thought Alec, I can't go skiing unless I have the money, but precious little Pooh can ask for the world and nobody bats an eye.

"Nobody told you how many presents to put on your list when you were six years old," Alec's mother whispered to him as she walked by.

"Nobody had to," said Alec. "I wasn't a greedy little pig."

The phone rang and Alec pounced on it. It was Cindy again.

"Hi, Alec," she said sweetly. "Can you come over? A bunch of us are going out sledding in the dark."

"Wow," said Alec. "That sounds great!"

"What sounds great?" asked Alec's mother.

Alec put his hand over the phone. "Cindy wants me to come over tonight —"

He hadn't even got the whole sentence out when his mother shook her head firmly.

"No, Alec," she said. "You've been out all afternoon, and it's a family night, remember? We're doing the gingerbread house."

"Yippie!" Stevie shouted.

Alec groaned. "C'mon, Ma," he pleaded, "you can do it without me. I'm not a little kid anymore."

Alec's mother shook her head once more. "Not open for discussion," she said.

Alec rolled his eyes up toward the ceiling. "I can't," he told Cindy disgustedly. "It's a *family* night."

"Okay," said Cindy, disappointment edging her voice. "I'll see you tomorrow then."

"You bet," said Alec. "Bye."

The garage door opened again and Kelly breezed in in her soccer uniform. Alec's father was a few steps behind.

"We won," Kelly stated matter-of-factly, as if making the announcement were only a formality.

Alec's parents gave each other quick hello kisses.

"Meg, you should have seen your daughter." Alec's father beamed. "She practically won the game single-handedly."

"That's super, honey," said Alec's mom. "Congratulations."

Alec's father turned to him. "Aren't you going to congratulate your sister, Alec?" he asked.

"Congratulations, Kel," said Alec, trying to sound genuinely enthused.

"Thanks," said Kelly. "So, what's for dinner? I'm starving."

"Corn dogs, Dino-fries, and baked beans," said Alec proudly. "I cooked it myself."

"Ugh!" said Kelly. "Grease City. Do you know how many calories are in a meal like that, let alone the fat and cholesterol?"

Alec rolled his eyes. "Well, it's better than the junk we have to eat when you cook."

"What's wrong with what I cook?"

"Tofu salad?" said Alec. "It looks like barf."

"That's enough, Alec," his mother interrupted. "We're about to eat, remember? Kelly, sit down. A meal like this won't hurt you once in a while."

"That's right," said Alec's father. "I think it was very nice of Alec to volunteer to cook."

Kelly wrinkled up her nose, but Alec noticed that she didn't turn anything down when the plates were passed.

"So," said Alec's father, "how did practice go, Alec?"

"I, uh, didn't have practice," said Alec. "It was canceled."

"Alec's father's brows came together. "Canceled? With a game on Monday?"

Alec could feel his ears starting to burn "Yeah," he said, his voice cracking a little. "I guess the coach was sick."

Alec's father regarded him intently. "I just saw Coach Costanzo at Kelly's game," he said. "He didn't look sick to me."

Alec swallowed the lump of corn dog in his mouth

with difficulty. He stared down at his plate, trying to think of what to say next.

"Alec?"

Alec raised his eyes to meet his father's.

"Practice wasn't canceled, was it?" said his father.

Alec shrugged.

"Answer me, Alec."

"No."

"Then why did you lie?"

Alec shrugged again.

"I want an answer, Alec."

"I don't know, Dad."

"You don't know what?"

"I don't know why I lied."

Alec's father's eyes burned into his. No one else breathed around the table. All the blood in Alec's body seemed to race to his head and scream in his ears.

"Why didn't you go to practice?" Alec's father asked.

"I hurt my knee in gym."

Alec saw the muscles of his father's jaw tighten. He saw the thoughts that raced through his father's head. Wimp, he was thinking. My son is a wimp.

Alec turned his eyes away.

"I won't tolerate lying, Alec," his father said, his voice low and even. "Your mother and I will talk after dinner and decide your punishment."

Alec nodded and took another bite of his corn dog. His mouth went through the motions of chewing and swallowing, but Alec didn't taste anything.

CHAPTER 8

Alec didn't say another word through the rest of dinner. At last Stevie asked to be excused and bolted off to play his video games.

Alec cleared his throat. "Can I be excused, too?" he asked.

His father nodded shortly.

Alec got up and started to walk away.

"Alec!" his father snapped.

Alec froze, wondering what he'd done now. "Yeah?" he asked.

"Clear your plate."

"But Stevie just —" Alec started to say, catching himself a little too late in the realization that this was not the time to discuss the inequities in the Lansing family chore structure.

"Stevie is six years old," Alec's father stated. "I expect

a little more from you than I do from him, but since you're so concerned, you can clear his plate as well."

Alec clamped his mouth shut and seethed in silence as he wiped up Stevie's ketchup-smeared placemat and carried his dish over to the sink.

"Oh," said Kelly suddenly. "I almost forgot: my report card!" She jumped up from the table, pulled a brown envelope out of her purse, and handed it to her father.

Alec felt the weight of another stone settling on his already-heavy heart. With the mood his father was in, he didn't relish getting into report cards.

"That's fantastic, Kelly," he heard his father say. "Look Meg, high honors again."

Alec's mother cooed over Kelly's report card, then turned and asked the inevitable question. . . .

"Alec? How about yours?"

Alec walked resignedly over to his notebook and opened it. He flipped through the pages all the way to the end. No report card. He flipped back again, his heart beating harder and faster, like a freight train picking up speed. He flipped through the pages once more, and then he knew with dreadful finality that his report card was gone. He thought back frantically and realized he must have lost it in the snowball fight. For a moment he considered running out the back door. It would be easier than trying to explain. But then his father was at his shoulder. Alec turned to face him, his mouth dry as cotton. "I lost my report card," he said, his voice barely louder than a whisper.

"You what?"

Alec saw the anger in his father's eyes and he was afraid, cold with fear right down to the tips of his toes. Tears sprang to his eyes and he hated himself for crying. He was too big to cry, but he couldn't help himself.

"I lost it, Dad," he repeated. "We had a snowball fight after school, and it must have fallen out of my notebook."

Alec's father started to breathe big, noisy breaths, in and out. "Do you expect me to *believe* that, Alec," he said, "after I caught you lying once already today?"

"It's true, Dad. I swear."

"Fine," said Alec's father, "fine. Then we're going to get into the car, and we're going to drive down to the schoolyard, and we're going to stay there until you find that card, understand?"

Alec sniffed and nodded. He wiped his eyes with the back of his hand.

"Now, John, be reasonable," said Alec's mother. "It's been snowing all day. He'll never find it."

Alec's father was already putting on his coat. "He'll find it," he said angrily. "He'll find it if he has to search every square inch of that yard on his hands and knees."

"John, now stop," said Alec's mother. Her voice was rising. "You're losing control and you're not making sense."

"I'm making sense. I'm making perfect sense," Alec's father bellowed. "It's your son that doesn't make any sense!"

Kelly slammed a dish towel down on the counter. "I *hate* this!" she shouted. "I can't stand it anymore!" Then she stormed out of the kitchen.

Stevie started to cry.

Alec's father hesitated, then pulled his coat off again and threw it across a chair. "Now look what you've done," he roared at Alec. "You've upset the whole family." He walked over and folded Stevie in his arms. "Don't cry, Stevie," he soothed. "It's okay. Everything is going to be all right."

Stevie sniffed loudly. "Don't be mad, Daddy." He sobbed. "Please don't be mad anymore."

Alec's father took a deep breath and hugged Stevie tighter. "It's all right," he repeated. "I'm not mad anymore."

"Are we still gonna do the gingerbread house?" Stevie asked, tears sliding down his cheeks.

Alec's father sighed, exchanged glances with Alec's mother, then nodded. "Yes," he said, "of course we are."

"Alec, too?" said Stevie.

Alec's father looked up at Alec and his eyes hardened. "No," he said quietly. "Alec is going to his room."

Alec swallowed and turned toward the hall.

Stevie started to cry again. "No," he whimpered. "I want Alec to help. Please, Daddy?"

"I'm sorry," Alec heard his father say, "but Alec doesn't deserve to be included in family night tonight."

Alec lay in the darkness of his room watching the snow swirl past the spotlights on the back of the house. Currents of wind swooped off the roof and played games with the snowflakes, so that sometimes it snowed sideways, and sometimes it snowed up, and sometimes the flakes seemed to stand perfectly still, tiny specks of stardust frozen in suspended animation. Alec slid his window open a crack, burrowed deeper into his blankets against the rush of pure, cold air, and listened to the silence of the woods filling up with snow. He emptied himself of everything, all feeling, all thought, and became one with the night, the soft, soothing, silent night.

"Alec?"

Alec had not heard his mother come in. He wrenched himself unwillingly back to reality and turned to look at her. She sat down beside him on the edge of the bed.

"You know, Alec," she said gently, "your father loves you very much."

Alec felt the tears come back to his eyes, but he said nothing. He didn't know. He didn't know anything anymore.

"He hates to be angry with you, Alec," his mother went on, "but he is very hurt by the fact that you lied."

Alec stared up at the slats of the bunk overhead and tried to swallow down the pain in his throat. "I didn't mean to lie," he said hoarsely. "I didn't really even think about it. It just seemed easier, that's all."

"Lying isn't easy, Alec. It's very hard. Sooner or later you forget: you trip up. Sooner or later the truth comes out, and then it's ten times worse than if you had just told the truth in the first place. Do you see that now?"

Alec nodded.

"Good," said his mother. "Then is there anything you'd like to tell me about your report card?"

Alec looked at her, uncomprehending.

"Like what?"

"Like what really happened to it."

Alec stiffened. "I told you what happened to it," he said.

His mother continued to look into his eyes. She seemed disappointed. "You're *sure*, Alec?"

"Yes, I'm sure. Don't you believe me?"

"I want to, Alec."

Alec turned and stared out the window again.

"How were your grades?" his mother asked.

"I didn't look."

"You didn't look?" Her voice seemed artificially strained, and Alex knew she didn't believe him, but there was nothing he could do about it. He'd lost her trust, and that hurt, but nothing he could say now would bring it back.

"No," he said simply, "I didn't look."

His mother sighed deeply. "All right," she said. "I guess we'll just have to wait and see on Monday. Right now, though, I think you owe your father an apology for lying. He's in with Stevie." She got up and walked to the door, then turned and looked back. "There will be no skiing tomorrow, Alec," she said quietly.

Alec's heart sank, but he knew better than to argue. He sighed and nodded. His mother disappeared, and he pushed back his covers and got out of bed. He walked slowly down the hall and stopped outside Stevie's room. He could hear his father's voice, gentle and comforting, reading Stevie a bedtime story. He closed his eyes a moment and drifted back, back to the days before Stevie had come between him and his father, back to the days when *he* was the one curled within the circle of that strong arm each night, drowsy and secure, wrapped in love.

Stevie's voice, high-pitched and whiny, shattered Alec's thoughts.

"Please, one more, Daddy, *please.*"

Alec grimaced. Spoiled little brat, he thought. Nothing was ever good enough for that kid. Alec stepped into the room. His father was bent over the bed, kissing Stevie good night. Stevie looked cozy, bathed in the glow of his night-light, surrounded by a bevy of stuffed animals, including, Alec noted ruefully, Cupcake the Bear, his own childhood favorite, whom Stevie had abducted years ago. Alec's father straightened up and looked at Alec.

For a brief moment Alec felt the urge to run to him and throw his arms around him and beg forgiveness the way he used to when he was little. Forgiveness had come easily then, in a rush of hugs and kisses. But that was then and this was now. Alec stood stiff and awkward, separated from his father by far more than the ten feet of carpet that stretched between them. He swallowed hard and pushed out the words that seemed to want to stick in his throat.

"I'm sorry, Dad."

His father nodded. "We'll start a new slate tomorrow, Alec," he said.

CHAPTER 9

The day dawned crystal white. The pines, laden with snow, reached up and touched a pale blue sky, tinged with pink. Alec looked longingly at the new black skis standing in the corner of his room. You didn't get many ski days like this in eastern Massachusetts. Clear skies, temps in the thirties, nine inches of new powder! He closed his eyes and pictured himself schussing down the slopes, expertly shifting from side to side, flying over jumps, doing daffies and back scratchers, maybe even a helicopter. He saw in his mind the breathtaking views from the top of Paquawket Mountain, the snow-covered slopes, the lake below, the hills of Massachusetts rolling north to meet the towering mountains of New Hampshire in the distance.

The phone rang, and Alec heard his mother answer it. "Alec," she yelled, "it's Muzzy."

Alec picked up the phone by his bed. "I can't go," he growled, even before Muzzy had a chance to say a word.

"What?" asked Muzzy incredulously. "Why not?"

"I just can't, that's all. I'll talk to you later."

Alec hung up the phone, and all his penitent feelings of the night before were washed away in a giant wave of self-pity. He got up, wrapped his quilt around himself, and trudged downstairs to watch cartoons.

"Good morning," said his mother as he passed through the kitchen.

Alec scowled and grunted in return.

"Don't you want some breakfast?" she called after him as he dragged his quilt down the hall to the family room.

"No," he grumbled.

"Alec," she went on, "you know how I feel about a good breakfast. You have to eat —"

"Later, Ma," Alec interrupted. "I'm not hungry now."

Stevie was already sprawled in front of the TV, deeply engrossed in playing a video game. Alec went over and shut the TV off.

"Idiot!" shrieked Stevie. He leaned over and bit Alec on his bare leg. Alec whacked him on the head.

"Mommy!" Stevie screamed. "Alec hit me."

"He bit me first," yelled Alec.

"He shut off my game," screamed Stevie.

"Alec!" yelled his mother. "There wasn't any trouble in there until you came down. Now cut it out."

Alec frowned. "Of course there wasn't any trouble," he

mumbled under his breath. "You think the little creep's gonna fight with himself?"

Stevie stuck his tongue out and put his game back on.

Alec whacked him on the back of the head again.

"Mommy!"

"I just barely touched him!"

"Alec, I'm warning you. If Stevie yells one more time . . ."

Stevie turned around and grinned at Alec. "Mommy!" he yelled.

"Alec, that's it! Go back up to your room."

"But I didn't touch him that time, Ma. I swear. He did that just to get me in trouble."

Alec's mother came to the family room door and stood staring at the two of them with her hands on her hips.

"I give up," she said. "I can't win with you two. One more word and you both go to your rooms and stay there for the rest of the day. Understand?"

Alec and Stevie both nodded contritely. As soon as she disappeared, Alec flicked Stevie in the ear with his finger. Stevie whirled, about to yell again, but Alec quickly put a finger to his lips.

"We'll *both* get punished, remember," he whispered.

Stevie grimaced, then tried to kick Alec in the stomach. Alec grabbed his leg and flipped him over. Stevie scrambled to his feet and charged again. Alec grabbed him, threw him down on the floor, and rolled over on top of him.

"Stop," Stevie gasped. "You're crushing me."

Alec laughed and sat up.

Stevie got to his feet and came at Alec once more, pounding with his small fists. Alec brushed the blows aside, grabbed Stevie around the neck, and flipped him effortlessly over on his back. Stevie lay there, his face beet red, his chest heaving. Tears of frustration filled his eyes.

"Crybaby," whispered Alec.

Suddenly Stevie was on his feet again, staring defiantly down at Alec.

"I'm telling," he declared.

"We'll *both* get in trouble," Alec warned.

Stevie narrowed his eyes. "No, we won't," he said, "because I'm telling about *yesterday*." He turned and dashed for the hall.

A knife plunged straight into Alec's heart. He jumped to his knees and lunged after Stevie. He caught hold of his ankle for a second by the doorway, but Stevie pulled free and ran toward the kitchen. Alec sank to the floor and stared after him. It was like watching the blade of a guillotine sliding downward toward his neck.

"Mommy," Stevie yelled.

The blade slid faster.

"Alec left me in the arcade yesterday,"

And faster.

"all alone,"

And faster.

"for a long time,"

And faster.

"and if Mrs. Franklin hadn't reminded him, he would have gone home without me."

SLAM!

Alec's head lay severed on the floor.

"*Alec!*"

Alec cringed and wished for a moment that he *was* dead. Unfortunately, he wasn't. He got slowly to his feet, wrapped his quilt around him again, and trudged out to the kitchen where the real executioners waited.

Alec's father had come down for breakfast and was sitting at the table with his mother. Stevie stood between them. The smug, triumphant look on his face made Alec's stomach turn.

It would have been easier if Alec's parents had been angry. Instead they looked hurt, and worried, and bewildered.

Alec's father sucked in a deep breath of air and let it out slowly. "Is this true, Alec?" he asked.

Alec looked down at the floor and nodded.

"Alec," said his mother, "how could you be so irresponsible? You promised me you wouldn't let him out of your sight. Don't you know what could've happened?"

Alec sighed heavily. "I only meant it to be for a minute, Ma, honest, but then there was this old lady —"

"There was no old lady," Stevie interrupted. "He went to talk to Cindy."

Alec glared at Stevie. "How would you know?" he snapped. "You weren't there. There *was* an old lady, and she almost fell down the stairs —"

"Alec!"

Alec turned back to his father. It was clear from the look in his eyes that he didn't believe a word Alec was saying.

"Alec, don't make things worse by lying again."

"I'm *not* lying, Dad."

Alec's father lowered his eyes and shook his head. "All right, Alec," he said quietly. "Just go to your room please."

"But Dad —"

"Just go, Alec."

Alec turned slowly and started toward the front hall.

"Do I have to give him the five dollars back?" Stevie asked.

Alec's heart banged against his chest.

"What five dollars?" he heard his mother ask.

"The five dollars he gave me when he made me promise not to tell."

Alec's heart sank slowly into the pit of his stomach.

"Alec."

His father's voice sounded tired and sad. Alec stopped and waited without turning around.

"Alec, you are grounded from now until New Year's Day. There will be no skiing, no dances, no movies, no phone calls, nothing. Is that understood?"

Alec swallowed hard and nodded.

"All right, then. Go to your room until lunchtime."

Alec started slowly up the stairs.

"Can I have my breakfast now, Mommy?" he heard Stevie ask sweetly behind him. Alec's stomach twisted into a knot of blind hatred. He bounded up the stairs into his room and slammed his door. He flung his quilt against the wall and kicked the jeans that were lying in the middle of his floor up into the air. Something fell out of the pocket and jingled as it hit the floor. Alec bent to pick it up. It was the old woman's trinket. He smiled bitterly and squeezed it in his hand.

"One wish," he said, winding up to fling the coin against the wall. "If I really had one wish it would be that precious little *Stevie* had never been born!"

CHAPTER 10

"Alec." It was his mother's voice, calling from downstairs. "I made some soup if you want some."

Alec folded his book and rolled off his bed. He dreaded going back downstairs, back to the tension and the anger, but he was starving after having skipped breakfast, and the smell of hot chicken-noodle soup was irresistible. He walked down and trudged sullenly into the kitchen. His mother was pulling toasted cheese sandwiches out of the toaster oven. She glanced at him absentmindedly.

"Hi, Pooh," she said, "where've you been all morning?"

Alec checked behind him for Stevie, but no one was there. He looked at his mother strangely. "Who are you talking to?" he asked.

His mother didn't seem to hear him. She whisked by and plopped the sandwiches on the table next to a stack of papers. "Oh," she said, as if it were an afterthought.

"The soup's on the stove. Help yourself, okay? I'm really in a rush." She shoved one of the sandwiches across the table toward Alec, bit into the other, and started poring over the papers.

Alec spooned up a bowl of soup, then walked over and sat down opposite his mother. She was wearing a nice wool suit, and he'd noticed that she had on high heels.

"Aren't you dressed kind of fancy for Christmas shopping?" he asked.

She scribbled something on one of the papers, then looked up at him and sighed dramatically. "Don't even *talk* to me about Christmas shopping," she said. "I get frantic whenever I think about it. I haven't even started, and I can't go today either. I have to run into the office and finish up the research on this Talbot case."

Alec looked over at her. "What office?" he asked.

His mother went back to scribbling notes. "*My* office," she said tiredly. "What office do you think I'd be talking about?"

Alec stared at her. "You have an office? Since when?"

Alec's mother looked up at him and frowned. "Alec, what is this, a game? You know I have an office. I've had an office for five years. Any more foolish questions?"

Alec shook his head and frowned back. "Yeah, how come nobody ever tells me anything around here?"

Alec's mother didn't answer. She finished her last bite of sandwich, then jumped up, pulled a briefcase off the counter, and stuffed the papers into it. "Be a good boy and pick up for me, will you, Pooh?" she asked. She started to put on her coat.

"Wait a minute," said Alec. "Where is everybody else?"

"Kelly's at soccer practice, and Dad went to the club."

"What club?"

"The *racquetball* club, Alec," his mother answered impatiently.

Alec was growing more and more confused. "The racquetball club?" he repeated. "What racquetball club?"

Alec's mother shook her head in exasperation. "Alec, I don't have time for this," she said. "With any luck I'll be home around five." She started toward the garage.

"Where's Stevie?" Alec yelled after her.

"Who?"

"Stevie?"

"Stevie who?"

Fear suddenly punched Alec sharply in the stomach and sent icy fingers crawling up his back. No, it couldn't be. Jumbled thoughts and images tumbled over one another in his mind. An old woman, a strange trinket, words spoken in anger. Perspiration broke out on his upper lip. No, it couldn't be. He jumped up and raced after his mother.

"Ma?"

"What, Alec?"

Alec stood staring at his mother. He was trembling inside. Then, with a rush of relief, it dawned on him what was happening. It was a trick. They had overheard him this morning and they were playing a trick on him, trying to teach him a lesson. He stopped trembling and started to smile.

"Okay, Ma," he said. "Where is he?"

Alec's mother did not look amused. "Where is who?" she asked sharply.

"Stevie," said Alec.

"Stevie *who?*" his mother repeated.

"Stevie, your son, my little brother? I know what kind of a game you're playing —"

"Well, I *don't* know what kind of a game *you're* playing, Alec," his mother interrupted. "All I know is, if I don't get to the office, I'm going to lose my trial on Monday. I'll see you this evening." She gave him a quick peck on the cheek and rushed out the door.

Alec watched her car pulling out of the driveway with a growing sense of dread. It couldn't be. It just couldn't be. He let his eyes sweep slowly around the family room. There were no Rat Pack guys lying on the floor, no Lego sculptures on the hearth. He walked over to Stevie's toy cupboard. He knelt down and pulled the door open. He heart slammed to a halt. The cupboard was full of old *National Geographic*s.

Alec's heart began to beat again, jerky and irregular. He fought for a breath. It couldn't be. It just couldn't. His heart was racing now. He jumped to his feet and bolted through the hall and up the front stairs. He grabbed onto the doorjamb of Stevie's room and stood staring. There was no bed, no Superman curtains, no Rat Pack posters on the wall. No toys, no books, no dirty clothes on the floor, nothing. Instead, there was a bright, flowered sofa, two matching pink chairs, and a TV.

Alec sank to his knees in the doorway and clasped his head in his hands. It was no game. They wouldn't go this far. Good Lord, what had he done?

Alec scrambled back to his feet and raced down the hall to his room. The talisman. He had to find the talisman. He searched everywhere: the floor, under the rug, behind the furniture. . . . There was no sign of the trinket. Then he went over and ran his hand slowly across the wall. There was no knick in the plaster where the coin should have hit. Come to think of it, there had been no sound. It hadn't occurred to him in his fit of anger, but now that he thought back, there *had not been* a sound. It was as if he had thrown the coin into thin air instead of against a solid plaster wall.

Alec began to sweat. Something strange was going on here. Something beyond his capacity to understand. He heard the garage door open again, and he rushed back downstairs. Kelly was just coming in from the garage.

"Kelly," he blurted desperately, "am I awake?"

Kelly grimaced at him. "What?"

"Am I awake? Tell me if I'm awake or if this is a dream."

Kelly's brows knitted together. She came over and looked closely into his eyes. "Are you *on* something, Alec?" she asked.

"Of course I'm not *on* anything. Just answer me, will you?"

Kelly shook her head and walked away. "Don't be stupid," she mumbled.

Alec ran after her and grabbed her arm. "Kelly, please, this is really important to me. Can you *prove* to me that I'm awake?"

Kelly stopped and stared at him. She chewed pensively for a moment on her bottom lip. "Prove to you that you're awake?" she repeated.

Alec nodded.

Kelly reached up and grabbed his nose and twisted it as hard as she could.

"Ow, ouch!" Alec screamed. He swatted her hand away and grabbed his nose. "What'd you do that for, you idiot?"

Kelly shrugged. "Did it hurt?" she asked.

"Of course it hurt."

"Then you're awake." She tossed her sweatshirt over her shoulder and walked out into the kitchen. Alec followed, rubbing his nose.

"Is that true?" he asked.

Kelly opened a cupboard and started rummaging through the boxes. "Is what true?"

"That you can't feel pain in your sleep?"

Kelly shoved a handful of Cheerios into her mouth and nodded.

Alec sat down at the table and stared at his cold soup. "Then I'm awake," he said slowly, "and it's all true."

Kelly loaded up her arms with bread and jelly and peanut butter and sat down across from him. "What are you mumbling about?" she asked.

Alec looked up at her. "We don't have a little brother, do we?" he asked.

Kelly screwed up her eyes and looked at him like he was crazy. "Alec, are you *sure* you're not on something?"

Alec rolled his eyes. "No, I'm not *on* something. I just asked a question, okay?"

"Alec, 'Do we have a little brother?' is not a normal question."

Alec was beginning to lose patience. "Look," he said, "just answer it, okay?"

Kelly threw up her hands. "Okay," she said. "We do *not* have a little brother, or a sister, or a cat or a dog. We don't even have a goldfish. All we have is you, me, Mom, and Dad. Okay?"

"Is Mom a lawyer already?" Alec went on.

"Already? What do you mean, already? It took her three years to get her law degree and she's been practicing for five years. Of course she's a lawyer."

"And is Dad still an engineer?"

Kelly raised her eyebrows. "Last time I asked," she said shortly. "Now, if you don't mind, I'm taking my lunch into the family room where I can eat in peace. She picked up the sandwich she had just made and stomped out of the kitchen.

Alec stared down at his cheese sandwich, poking holes in it thoughtfully with his fork. Then suddenly he hurled the fork across the kitchen and buried his face in his hands.

CHAPTER 11

Alec held the receiver in his hand and stared at the phone. He chewed his lip, checked the number in the phone book for the fifteenth time, sucked in a deep breath, and started to press the numbers. He put the receiver to his ear and listened, his heart beating faster with every ring.

"Hello?" a man's voice answered.

"Is —" Alec's voice cracked and he had to begin again. "Is Abbey Bennett home?" he squeaked.

"Just a minute."

The phone in Alec's hand was slippery from the sweat of his palm.

"Hello!"

The cheery voice startled Alec, and the phone slid out of his hand, bounced off the kitchen counter, and clattered to the floor. Alec scrambled after it, dropping it a couple more times in his haste.

"Hello, hello," he said at last, breathing in gasps into the phone.

"Yes, hello," came the cheery voice again.

"I'm sorry about that," Alec apologized. "I dropped the phone."

There was a laugh. "That's okay. Who is this anyway?"

"Uh, it's . . . Alec Lansing."

There was a silence.

"We met at the mall yesterday, remember?" Alec hurried on.

More silence.

"You know my sister, Kelly Lansing," Alec continued.

"Oh, right," said the voice. "Alec, sure I know who you are, but . . . I didn't see you at the mall yesterday."

Alec's heart sank. "You didn't?"

"No, I was out there, but . . . Well, anyway, what did you call for?"

"Oh, uh . . ." Alec's ears started to burn. "Uh, just, nothing. Just to tell you my sister says hi."

"Oh?" There was a little amused laugh. "Well, okay, thanks. Tell her I said hi, too."

"Okay," said Alec, "bye."

"Bye, Alec."

Alec hung up the phone and shook his head. "Boy, did I make a jerk of myself," he mumbled.

"So what else is new?" Kelly appeared from around the corner.

"You were listening?" Alec snapped.

"Not on purpose." Kelly's eyes danced. "What are you doing calling Abbey Bennett? She's my age."

Alec scowled. "None of your business, butt head." He stomped into the family room and threw himself down on the couch. He started cracking his knuckles and thinking. He mustn't have met Abbey because he didn't have to take Stevie to Toy Town. In fact, he mustn't have even had a fight with Cindy, because if Stevie didn't exist, he couldn't have said anything to her. But Alec still must have met the old woman somehow, or how could he have gotten the talisman? It was all too confusing, but he did know one thing. Somehow he had to find that old woman again.

Alec heard the hum of an engine and looked out the family room window.

"Hey," he shouted to Kelly, "do we know anybody with a red Porsche?"

"Very funny, Alec," came Kelly's reply.

"What do you m —" Alec stopped mid-sentence. The Porsche pulled up and parked in the driveway, and he watched with his mouth open as his father got out of the driver's seat.

"Holy . . . Kelly!"

"What?"

"Has Dad got a Porsche?"

"Alec, are you starting that again?"

Alec didn't answer. He tore out of the door to the garage, nearly bowling his father over on the way.

"Alec, what the —?"

"Oh, wow," was all Alec could say. "Oh, wow, this car is *awesome*, Dad."

Alec's father gave him a quizzical smile.

"Alec, we've had this car for over a year. Why the sudden fuss?"

"We have? Oh, wow. Wow! Can we go for a drive? Can I back it out of the driveway? Look at that dashboard! Oh, this is *awesome*. I can't believe it. Wow."

Kelly stuck her head out of the door, and Alec's father turned to look at her. "Do you have any idea what this is all about?" he asked her.

Kelly shook her head. "I think he's been smoking something, Dad," she said. "He's been bonkers all afternoon."

Alec's father's brows knitted together, and he walked over to Alec.

"Alec," he said, "let me look at your eyes."

Alec was too excited to stand still. He kept jumping in and out of the car, pressing all the buttons, turning all the knobs, looking under the hood, opening the trunk.

"Alec," his father kept saying more and more insistently. "Alec! Stand still!" He grabbed Alec by the arm and stared hard into his eyes.

"I'm okay, Dad," Alec tried to assure him. "Honest. It's just that —"

"Just what, Alec?"

Alec stared back at him. What was he supposed to say? Just that I traded my little brother in for a Porsche? He shook his head. "Nothing, Dad," he said. "I just got a little carried away — that's all."

His father continued to stare at him. "Come on in the house," he said. "I think we'd better have a talk."

Alec followed his father reluctantly, turning several times to look again at the Porsche.

"Alec!"

"I'm coming, I'm coming."

"What's been going on here?" Alec's father asked Kelly when they got to the kitchen.

"Beats me," said Kelly. "He's been asking questions like 'Do we have a little brother?' and 'Is Mom a lawyer already?' and he's been calling up girls my age."

"*One* girl," Alec corrected her.

Alec's father pulled him over to the window and looked into his eyes again.

"Alec," he asked, "did you . . . take anything?"

Alec pulled away. "Of course not," he said resentfully. His father didn't look convinced.

"You're sure, Alec?"

"Yes, I'm sure. You know me better than that."

Alec's father raised an eyebrow. "You'd better be telling me the truth," he warned.

"Dad, trust me," said Alec. Then he flashed a wide, innocent grin.

His father gave a cynical snort, then smiled and shook his head. "I'm going up to take a shower," he said. "Then I'm going out to do a little Christmas shopping. What are you two up to this afternoon?"

"I'm going over to Darleen's," said Kelly. She looked at Alec as if waiting for his answer.

"I'm . . ." Alec hesitated. He was about to say *grounded till New Year's.* But then he remembered. If there was no Stevie, then there couldn't have been any fight, so he *wasn't* grounded. And with all the other changes that had taken place, maybe he wasn't even forbidden to go skiing anymore. It was worth a try. "Going skiing?" he finished tentatively.

His father nodded matter-of-factly and walked out of the kitchen.

"Awesome," Alec whispered.

"What's awesome?" asked Kelly.

"Oh . . . uh . . . the Porsche," he said quickly. "That's sure an awesome car."

Kelly snorted. "You're weird, Alec," she said.

Alec grinned innocently. Suddenly he had another thought. "Hey, Kel," he whispered excitedly, "have we got anything else?"

Kelly narrowed her eyes. "What?"

"I mean like boats, or skimobiles, or motorcycles, or anything?"

Kelly stared at him apprehensively. "Cut it out, Alec," she said. "You're really starting to scare me."

CHAPTER 12

Alec put away his skis and boots, then unzipped his ski coat and hung it up in the back hall closet. His cheeks stung as the heat of the house warmed them. He sniffed as he walked into the kitchen and grabbed a tissue to wipe his nose.

"Well," said his father, who was stirring some soup or something on the stove, "don't you look exhilarated. Did you have a good day on the slopes?"

"Awesome," said Alec. "It was the best." He looked around. "Mom home yet?"

His father shook his head. "She called to say she wouldn't be here till around seven."

Alec nodded, then looked around again. Something was missing. What was it? Then he realized. The Christmas trimmings. They were all gone. He walked out into the front hall and peered into the living room. The tree was gone, too.

"Where are the Christmas decorations?" Alec asked as he walked back out into the kitchen.

His father glanced up from the stove. "In the attic," he said. "Why?"

"Well, when are we gonna put them up?" Alec asked. "Christmas is only a week away."

Alec's father shrugged. "Soon, I guess. Maybe tomorrow."

"Can we get the tree tomorrow, too?" Alec asked.

"Get? You mean get it down from the attic?" Alec's father mumbled absentmindedly. "Sure, I don't see why not."

Get it down from the attic? Alec's heart sank. An artificial tree? They had an artificial tree? Why? What could have made them change their minds? His mother had always sworn that she'd never, ever, have an artificial tree.

"But . . . don't we, I mean, can't we get a real tree?"

Alec's father frowned. "Of course not," he said. "I paid two hundred and fifty dollars for that tree upstairs. Why would I shell out another fifty or sixty for some needle-dropping nuisance?"

"But —"

"Forget it, Alec."

Kelly walked into the kitchen. "Forget what?"

"Alec's got it in his head that he wants a real tree this year," Alec's father told her.

Kelly snorted. "Too much work," she said. Then she grinned. "I thought you all might like to skip Christmas this year and send me on a trip to the Bahamas instead."

Alec's father laughed, then winked at Alec and Kelly. "Can you both keep a secret?" he asked.

They nodded.

Alec's father took his pot off the stove and gestured for them to follow. He led them upstairs to what used to be Stevie's room. Alec got a strange, sinking feeling when he saw it again. He'd been trying all day not to think too much about Stevie.

Alec's father pushed the closet door open. In place of Stevie's toys and little, short clothes, was a neat row of garment bags. He unzipped one and pulled something heavy and dark out of it.

Kelly shrieked and reached out to touch it. "A *mink!*" she squealed. "You bought Ma a mink!"

Alec's father grinned proudly.

"Oh, she'll love it," Kelly went on, then she giggled wickedly. "Madeleine Blackwell will just be *green*. She made such a big deal out of getting that silver fox."

Alec's father gave them both a conspiratorial wink. "We can't have the neighbors dressing better than your mother, can we?" he said.

"I can't *wait* to see her face," said Kelly, giggling again.

"Mom's?" asked Alec.

"No," said Kelly, "Madeleine's."

"But . . ." Alec was confused. "I thought Mom didn't approve of killing animals to make furs."

Kelly gave Alec a smug look. "I think she'll get over that pretty quick when she sees this," she said.

Alec frowned. "I thought Mom was upset when Mrs. Blackwell got that coat."

Kelly and Alec's father looked at each other and laughed. "Yeah," said Kelly, "and Mrs. Blackwell will be upset when Mom gets *this* one." Alec's father returned the coat to the bag, then he and Kelly went back downstairs, still laughing together. Alec sat down a moment on the flowered couch, wondering. What was all that about keeping up with the neighbors? That didn't sound like his parents. And a mink? He hoped his mother was as happy as Kelly and his dad expected. She usually hated people spending a lot of money on her, and . . . he could have sworn he'd heard her say she'd never wear a fur. . . .

"Alec," Kelly yelled from downstairs, "your night to set the table."

Alec sighed and pushed himself up out of the couch. It seemed like Stevie's disappearance had changed more around here than cars and furniture. But why?

Alec's father was at the stove again.

"What are you making?" Alec asked.

"Béarnaise."

"Bear what?"

"Béarnaise sauce, Alec, for the filet."

"For the what?"

Alec's father frowned. "Just set the table, Alec."

Alec went over and started pulling dishes out of the cupboard.

"Alec," his father interrupted, "what *are* you doing?"

Alec paused, dishes in hand. "I'm setting the table."

Alec's father shook his head. "It's *Saturday* night, Alec."

Alec waited, expecting his father to say more, but he didn't. "So?" Alec prompted.

Alec's father shook his head impatiently. "So we eat in the dining room on Saturday nights, remember?"

Alec's mouth fell open. "We do?"

His father arched an eyebrow.

"Oh, yeah," Alec said quickly. "I forgot." He pushed the dishes back into the cupboard.

"Use the blue damask," his father said.

Alec nodded, pretending to understand. Then Kelly walked by, and he followed her into the family room.

"Where's the blue damask?" he whispered.

Kelly eyed him strangely. "Where it always is."

Alec sighed. "Okay, smarty," he said, "*what* is the blue damask?"

"The blue *tablecloth*," said Kelly, as if Alec had just asked the world's stupidest question.

"Oh." Alec walked into the dining room and pulled open the linen drawer. "So why didn't he just *say* table-cloth?" he mumbled to himself.

Alec spread the cloth on the dining room table, then opened the china cabinet.

"How many should I set it for?" he yelled.

"Just us," his father yelled back.

"Not me," Kelly put in. "I'm outta here."

Alec waited, expecting his father to give Kelly some kind of hassle about going out again after being gone all day, but nothing further was said. Alec opened the china cabinet and let out a low whistle.

"You sure you want me to use this fancy stuff?" he yelled.

"Yes, Alec," his father answered tiredly.

Alec handled the delicate china and crystal gingerly. Something told him he might find himself in more trouble than usual if he broke a dish tonight. He frowned. Sure seemed like a lot of fuss for "just us." He finished setting the table, then went back out into the kitchen and watched in astonishment as his father continued to prepare a full gourmet meal. The father he remembered hardly knew how to scramble an egg.

It got to be seven o'clock. Alec's father poured himself a glass of wine and glanced irritably at the clock.

"Late again," he mumbled.

Alec's mother finally pulled into the driveway at about seven-thirty. She walked into the kitchen, shoulders drooping. "I'm exhausted," she groaned, kicking off her heels and dropping her briefcase on the counter. "I never thought I'd get done in time."

Alec's father frowned. "It's always some kind of a crisis, isn't it?" he muttered.

"What did you say?" asked Alec's mother.

"I said . . . the béarnaise is curdled," Alec's father snapped.

Alec's mother glanced at the clock. "Oh, dear." She grimaced. "I'm sorry. I must have lost track of the time."

"Never mind," said Alec's father. "Just go get changed."

CHAPTER 13

Alec's mother came back into the kitchen a short while later, knotting the belt on her lounging pajamas.

"Who set the dining room table?" she asked.

"I did," said Alec.

Alec's mother shook her head and gave him a bemused smile.

"Something wrong?" Alec's father asked.

"Come see."

Alec followed his parents into the dining room. What was the problem, he wondered? Everybody had a plate, a glass, a napkin, and a pile of silverware.

Alec's father glanced at the table, then cast a disgruntled eye at Alec, but said nothing.

Alec's mother went around rearranging the whole table, folding the napkins into little triangles that stood up, straightening the dishes, separating the silverware, and adding more dishes and utensils than Alec knew what to do with. At last they all sat down, and Alec's father served the first course, some kind of creamy white soup. Alec carefully chose the correct utensil and took a tentative spoonful.

"Ach!" he said. "This stuff is ice cold."

His mother gave him a puzzled glance. "Of course it is, Alec," she said matter-of-factly. "It's vichyssoise."

Alec surmised from the tone of her voice that vichyssoise, whatever it was, was a fairly common item on their menu these days.

"Oh, yeah," he said, giving a nervous little laugh. "I, uh, thought it was cream of mushroom for a minute there." He put another spoon of the gluey, cold soup in his mouth and tried not to gag as he swallowed it down.

They ate quietly for a while. Then Alec's mother suddenly clasped her hands wistfully under her chin. "You know what I wish?" she said.

"What?" asked Alec's father.

"I wish we could just drop everything and go up to the condo for the day tomorrow. It would be so beautiful with all this snow."

Alec nearly choked. "C-condo!" he blurted.

Alec's parents exchanged glances, but Alec was too excited to pay any heed.

"Wh-what condo?" he asked.

Alec's mother frowned. "Alec, are you still playing that crazy game from this morning? You know very well we only have one condo."

Alec looked from one parent to the other.

"Oh, yeah," he said. "Of course. The condo at uh . . . uh . . ."

"Thunder Mountain," his mother filled in.

"Thunder Mountain!" Alec jumped up and punched his fist triumphantly in the air. "Yes!" he shouted. "We have a condo at Thunder Mountain Ski Resort!"

There was absolute silence around the table. Alec's mom stared at his dad. "What is going on here?" she asked.

"Alec appears to be suddenly very grateful for all the nice things he has in life," his father answered.

Alec's mother looked up at him suspiciously. He felt himself turning red.

"Alec, sit down and eat," she said quietly.

Alec slid sheepishly back into his chair.

"As I was saying," his mother went on, "I would love to go up there tomorrow."

"So let's do it," his father answered.

Alec's mother sighed. "I can't," she said. "I haven't even started the Christmas shopping."

Alec's dad waved her words away. "So what?" he said. "The kids aren't babies anymore. We'll give them the money and let them buy their own gifts."

Alec swallowed down another lump of soup. "Our own gifts?" he repeated.

"Sure," said his father. "That way you'll get just what you want."

"You mean," said Alec, "no . . . Santa Claus?"

Alec's mom put her hand over her mouth to hide a smile.

"I mean . . ." Alec could feel himself blushing again. "Not for me, but what about . . . ?" He got a sudden sinking feeling in his chest and couldn't go on. What about Stevie? he was thinking. Stevie and his Wish Book, and his never-ending list. Stevie, too excited to go to sleep on Christmas Eve. Stevie shivering with excitement at the top of the stairs on Christmas morning. Was all that gone forever?

"Alec?" His mother wasn't smiling anymore. She studied his face a moment, then reached across the table and patted his hand.

"No," she said, in answer to Alec's father's suggestion. "I don't think our Pooh is ready to be quite that grown up."

Alec frowned. "Of course I am," he snapped. "And don't call me Pooh! I'm *not* Pooh."

CHAPTER 14

Alec lay back in the hot tub on the deck of the condo. His muscles were gloriously tired from a whole day on the slopes. It was snowing very lightly, just flurries, but it was beautiful to be out there, in the night, his body immersed in warm water and snowflakes landing on his lashes. The flakes were large, and they made a little *thwip, thwip, thwip* sound as they touched the steamy water and disappeared.

Alec had never dreamed that life could be so rich. He wanted to be happy. He should be happy, but the initial numbing bewilderment he had felt at all the amazing changes in his life was slowly ebbing away, being replaced by a growing dread, a deepening sense that something was terribly wrong. All day long he'd been on an emotional roller coaster. From elation to sorrow, exhilaration to fear. Whenever he'd felt a surge of wonder, of joy, it was quickly followed.by a stab of guilt and pain, and a single thought: Stevie.

Alec heard the patio door slide open, and his mother stepped out onto the deck in her robe and bathing suit. She dropped her robe on a chair next to Alec's and slid quickly into the water beside him. She had a cup of hot chocolate in her hand, and she offered him a sip. Alec shook his head, and she took a drink herself.

"Mmmm," she said. "When I'm up here I never want to go home."

Alec looked around him and nodded. "I can see why."

Alec's mother leaned back and closed her eyes and let the snowflakes collect on her face. "This is the only place I can relax," she murmured.

Alec looked at her with concern. She seemed thinner than she used to be, and the worry lines on her face were deeper. "Do you like working, Ma?" Alec asked.

His mother opened her eyes again and looked at him. "Of course I do," she said. "Why do you ask?"

Alec shrugged. "I don't know," he said. "I was just kind of wondering if you ever wished you'd waited a little longer and maybe had another child before you went back to school."

Alec's mother gave him a puzzled smile. "That's a funny question from you, Alec," she said. "Why do you ask?"

Alec shrugged. "I don't know," he said. "I guess I just wonder how it would be sometimes, to have a little . . . brother or something."

Alec's mother seemed surprised by his answer. She smiled, then lay back and stared up at the sky. "Well," she said, "to be honest, I guess I've wondered, too. I think all women do. Sometimes I even dream that I'm pregnant, or that we have a new baby, and then when I wake up and find it isn't true, I feel kind of empty inside, almost, for a second, as if I'd had another child and lost it."

Alec felt a sharp stab in his heart. His mother was silent for a while, but then she reached over and rubbed his short hair.

"But," she went on, "I'm not sorry. Not really. Your father and I discussed having a third child long ago, and we both decided that we'd rather get on with our careers and be able to provide a really nice lifestyle for you and Kelly." She gestured toward the mountain and smiled. "That's why we have all this."

Alec nodded thoughtfully. That made sense. He never *had* understood why his parents would want a third child. Maybe it wasn't all so bad then, if his parents were happy. And if Stevie had never existed, then Stevie would never know the difference. But . . . the sinking feeling returned. . . . Stevie *had* existed.

"Alec?" His mother was staring at him again. "Is something wrong?"

Alec shook his head. "No," he said. "I . . . was just wondering about something else."

"Oh? What's that?"

"Well . . . ," Alec swallowed hard and went on, "do

. . . do you think it would be the same as killing someone if you could fix it so they were never born?"

Alec's mother stared at him for a second. Then her eyes flew wide.

"My God," she said. "Alec, is there a girl? Is she . . ? You didn't . . ? You couldn't . . . You're only thirteen! Oh, Lord, is that why you've been acting so strangely?"

Alec suddenly realized what she was thinking. "No, *no*, Ma!" he cried, his cheeks burning. "Nothing like that. Jeez!"

"Well, what on earth *are* you talking about then?"

Alec sank down into the water. "Nothing. Honest. It was . . . uh . . . an essay question we had in social studies."

"*Oh!*" Alec's mother looked immensely relieved.

Alec slowly let out a big breath. "I think I'll go in now," he said. He climbed out of the tub and put on his robe. His father was just coming out.

"Have you seen Kelly, Dad?" Alec asked.

"She's still down in the family room, sulking about having to come along today."

Alec slid the door shut. He took a towel off the rack and walked downstairs rubbing his head. Kelly was watching *Rainman*, that movie starring Dustin Hoffman and Tom Cruise. It was about some guy who was trying to get his autistic brother to hang out with him and be his friend, like a normal brother.

Alec frowned. Of all the movies they had in their video

library, why did she have to be watching that one? "What have you got that on for?" he snapped.

Kelly looked up at him and scowled. "What's your problem?" she asked.

"Nothing," said Alec, "but don't you ever get sick of that stupid movie?"

"It's not stupid," said Kelly, "and no, I don't get sick of it. I could watch Tom Cruise every day of my life, if it's any of your business."

Alec stood in the doorway, watching Tom Cruise trying to teach his retarded brother to dance. A lump rose in his throat. He used to have a brother. A normal, healthy brother. And he'd wished him away.

Alec swallowed the lump down. He stomped over and shut off the VCR.

"Hey!" Kelly shouted. "What are you doing?"

"I don't want to watch that movie right now, okay?" Alec shouted.

"No, it's not okay!" Kelly jumped up and went to turn the TV back on. Alec grabbed her arm.

"Let me go, Alec," she cried, trying to pull away.

Alec squeezed tighter, anger building inside him.

"Alec!" Kelly looked into his eyes. Then she suddenly backed down. She pulled her arm away and rubbed it. She narrowed her eyes. "What's *wrong* with you, Alec?" she asked, her voice low and troubled.

Alec swallowed hard again. "I don't know."

Kelly took hold of his sleeve. She pulled him over to the couch, pushed him down, and sat beside him.

"Alec, how could you do this?" she whispered.

Alec looked at her and his heart raced. "You know?"

"Of course I know. Alec, I thought you were smarter than this. I know Mom and Dad can be a pain sometimes, and I know you worry about school, but drugs aren't the answer, Alec. Please, you've got to stop, or I'll have to tell Mom and Dad."

Alec threw his head back and sank down on the couch. "It's not *drugs!*" he said through clenched teeth.

"Alec, trust me —"

"No!" Alec sat back up and stared at Kelly. "You trust *me,* okay? I haven't changed. I'm the same person I always was. I don't do drugs! Nobody around here understands anything."

Kelly's voice rose. "If it's not drugs, then what is it, Alec? What are we supposed to understand?"

Alec stared hard into her eyes, wanting to tell her, but then he turned away. "Nothing," he said, "never mind." He stood up. "Wanna take a walk?"

"Not especially."

"Why not?"

"I just don't, okay? It's cold out. I don't even want to be here."

Alec frowned and stalked out of the room. Stevie would have gone with him. Stevie wouldn't have cared how cold it was. Alec went to his room and put his sweats on. He slipped into his parka and went outside. He climbed partway up the mountain, then stopped and stood in the soft, snowy night, staring down at the twinkling lights in the valley below. It was so beautiful here. If only he could be happy. If only . . .

Somewhere down below he heard shouts and laughter. A bunch of little kids were playing hide-and-seek in the dark. Alec pressed his lips together and hung his head. Stevie would have loved it here.

CHAPTER 15

They were late getting home, and Alec overslept the next morning as usual, but nobody seemed to care. His mother had already left for work when he came down to breakfast, and his father seemed engrossed in the newspaper. Only Kelly took any notice of him at all.

"Got a game today?" she asked as she munched on a chocolate Pop Tart.

Alec tensed and glanced at his father. He would rather that his father not be reminded of the game. He'd be sure to show up if he knew, and having his father in the stands was what made Alec the most nervous about playing. If his father had heard, though, he showed no sign. He continued staring at the financial columns.

Alec nodded shortly to Kelly and tried to change the subject. "How come you're so into junk food all of a sudden?" he asked, nodding at her Pop Tart.

Kelly gave him a puzzled glance and ignored his question. "What time is it?" she asked.

Alec stretched his neck back and looked at the clock. Seven-fifteen! "Holy cow," he said, "I just missed the bus!"

Kelly shook her head. "I'm driving," she said tiredly.

"Driving? Oh, yeah . . ." Alec had forgotten that his father's Buick belonged to Kelly now.

"I meant," Kelly went on impatiently, "what time is the *game?* I can see the clock myself."

"Oh." Alec laughed nervously and glanced again at his father, who simply turned a page and went on reading.

"Four," said Alec, jumping up quickly from the table. "We'd better get going."

"All right," said Kelly, "but I don't know what the big rush is."

"Bye, Dad," Alec called.

His father glanced up and nodded. Kelly walked out of the kitchen without a word. Alec waited. She walked back in again.

"Are you coming or not?" she asked impatiently.

"Well . . . yeah," said Alec. "Are you ready to go?"

"Sure I'm ready. Why wouldn't I be?"

"Well, you didn't kiss Dad good-bye or anything."

Kelly looked over at her father. "Why should I? Is he going on a trip?"

Alec looked at her. "No," he said, "but you always . . . I mean you used to . . . I mean, won't he . . ?"

Alec looked over at his father, unconcernedly sipping

coffee and turning the pages of his paper. He was like a stranger.

Alec shook his head. "Never mind," he said quietly. He started to follow Kelly out of the room, but then he turned back.

"Bye, Dad," he called.

His father looked up. "Oh, bye Alec," he said. "And good luck this afternoon. Knock 'em dead."

Alec's heart sank. Kelly and her big mouth!

Alec felt like he was dragging a lead weight around all day. With everything else he had on his mind, the last thing he wanted to do was go through the torture of a basketball game. With any luck the coach wouldn't put him in. But then Alec's father would be disappointed. Or would he? He hadn't actually said he was coming. Alec sighed. Who was he trying to kid? Wild horses couldn't keep his father away from one of his games.

In the locker room that afternoon, Alec dallied over getting dressed for the game. He tried to think of some way out of having to walk into that gym.

"Hurry up, Giraffe," yelled Will Johnston. "We wouldn't want the bench to get cold." Will was the best all-around athlete in the school, and he took great pleasure in pointing out Alec's deficiencies every chance he got.

Muzzy had come to watch the game, and he leaned against a locker, waiting for Alec to get dressed. "Don't listen to him," he told Alec. "He's just jealous."

Alec snorted. "Of what?"

"Of you, because you're prettier than he is, and all the ladies like you, 'cause you're an okay dude."

Alec laughed. "Right," he said cynically. He stuffed his clothes into his locker and headed for the gym.

Muzzy followed, one step behind. "I wouldn't kid you, man," he insisted. "I don't know why you always think I'm jivin' ya."

Alec wasn't listening. The moment of agony had arrived. He walked out into the gym. There was a sudden hush, and the coach of the visiting team went pale. His players began to whisper together. There were catcalls from the bleachers of "Hey, who's the ringer?" and "That kid's no eighth-grader!" They all stared at Alec as he walked across the floor. He knew he should be used to it by now. It happened every game, but it still jangled his nerves. His ears started to burn, and it took all his concentration to pick up his feet and put them down, one after the other, without tangling them in his long legs. At last he reached the refuge of the bench and dropped down heavily, hunching over to try and hide himself among the shorter players. He glanced quickly over his shoulder at his father's customary seat in the stands. It was empty. He scanned the stragglers still coming in through the gym doors. His father wasn't among them either.

Strange, thought Alec. His father was never late.

"All right guys, listen up," said Coach Costanzo. "Here's the starting lineup."

Alec tensed.

"Johnston, Marconi, White, Fisher, and Lavitski," the coach called out. Alec breathed a sigh of relief. Now if he could just manage to stay out of the coach's sight for the rest of the game. That wasn't easy. He hunched forward and tried to make himself as inconspicuous as possible. The game started. Alec stared down at his feet and listened to the *squeak, squeak, squeak* of sneakers on wood and the hollow sound of the basketball dribbling up and down the court and bouncing off the backboards. The first quarter dragged by, then the second. The score was tight and there were few substitutions. Alec turned a couple of times to look for his father. He was nowhere to be seen. Something must have come up at the office, Alec told himself. Good. One less thing to worry about.

Late in the third quarter there was a collision under the boards, and two of Alec's teammates got hurt.

"Lansing," yelled the coach.

Alec took a deep breath. Why couldn't his luck have held out just a little longer? He got up and loped unenthusiastically out onto the floor. At least he wouldn't have to deal with his father cheering over every stupid move he made.

"Watch out," someone on the opposing bench called out. "Here comes their secret weapon."

Will Johnston snorted. Sweat soaked through his jersey and dripped from his hair. He gave Alec an icy glare. "Just don't screw up," he warned as he started dribbling. Alec sprinted up court, easily outstriding Will, and took his position under the basket. Will passed. Alec reached up, but before he could get a hand on the ball a little guard from the other team swooped in from nowhere and snatched it right out of the air. He heard a collective groan from the stands.

Alec's face burned. He hated this so much. Why was he out here doing this to himself? He loped down court after the guard. The guard aimed and shot. The ball whirled around the rim and bounced off.

"Get it, Lansing! Get the rebound!" Coach Costanzo shouted.

Alec stepped back and reached up. The ball was still too high. He stepped back farther. Then suddenly his legs got all tangled up in someone else's. There was a thump, and Alec staggered over someone, staggered a few more steps, nearly fell, righted himself, reached out, and, miracle of miracles, caught the ball in his hands.

The stands went crazy, and Alec, buoyed by their enthusiasm, whirled and started dribbling up the court. The next thing he knew, he was all alone in the opponent's territory.

"Shoot! Shoot!" everyone shouted. Alec's heart raced. He aimed, shot, then closed his eyes and prayed. The roar that went up from the crowd told him the shot was good.

"EEEYess!" Alec shouted, jumping up and punching triumphantly at the air. Instinctively he whirled and looked to the stands for his father's reaction.

Then he remembered.

Will Johnston ran by and whacked him on the rump.

"Not bad, Lansing," he said. "Never knew you had it in you." Alec smiled, trying to let Will's praise and the approval of the crowd be enough. It didn't matter that his father wasn't there. It really didn't.

CHAPTER 16

It was dark when the game ended. Kelly was waiting out in the parking lot.

"We won," Alec announced as he slid into the front seat of the Buick. "Fifty-six to forty-eight. I got a basket!"

"Good," said Kelly, sounding as bored as she looked. She turned the wheel and guided the car out of the lot.

They drove in silence for a while. Alec looked at the houses along the way. Their living rooms glowed warm and inviting, Christmas trees and lighted menorahs winking in the windows.

"Dad didn't come," Alec said quietly.

"What?" asked Kelly.

"Dad didn't come," Alec repeated, a little more loudly. "He didn't come to the game."

"Did he say he would?" asked Kelly.

"Well, no," said Alec, "but he usually . . . I mean he

used to . . . I mean, doesn't he usually go to your games?"

"No," said Kelly.

Alec couldn't believe his ears. "He doesn't? You mean, never?"

Kelly shrugged. "No, not *never*. He makes one every now and then. Why?"

Alec didn't answer. *Every now and then?* What on earth could have happened to make his father lose interest in their sports? The father he knew would sooner lose interest in breathing. Why, he used to go into the office at the crack of dawn sometimes, just so he could get his work done in time to make a game.

"But . . . he used to love to go to our games when we were little," Alec mused.

Kelly laughed. "Well, we're not little anymore, Alec. And Dad's been awful busy since he got that last promotion. What's the big deal?"

Alec turned to stare out the window again. "Nothing," he said quietly. Kelly was right. It was no big deal.

CHAPTER 17

Alec's father was watching *Wall Street Week* when they got home.

"We won," Alec told him.

"Won what?" asked his father absently.

"The basketball game."

"Oh, right. *Great!* Tell me about it at dinner, okay, sport? This is important."

Alec nodded. "Sure."

"Is it my night to cook?" Kelly asked.

Alec's father nodded.

"Pizza okay?"

"Damn," said Alec's father.

"What?" asked Kelly.

"Huh?" Alec's father looked up. "Oh, nothing. Just a stock I bought last week. It's doing lousy. Pizza's fine. Just fine." He went back to staring at the TV.

Alec set the table while Kelly cooked. Their mother breezed in just as Kelly was pulling the finished pizzas out of the oven.

"Oh, good," she said. "I'm so glad you made something quick. I have a lot of work to do tonight."

"Dinner's ready, Dad," Kelly yelled.

Their father came out scowling.

"What's wrong with you?" Alec's mom asked.

"Dow Jones," his father grumbled. "If it doesn't turn around soon, we'll all be in the poor house."

Alec's mother shook her head. "Maybe *you* will," she teased. "*My* money's in the bank."

Alec's ears perked up. *Her* money? Since when did his mother and father have separate accounts?

Alec's father snorted. "Nobody ever got rich on bank interest," he said.

His mother smiled wryly. "Maybe not, but nobody ever had a heart attack worrying about it either."

Alec's father grimaced and stuffed a bite of pizza in his mouth.

"We won our game," Alec said, unable to hold his news in any longer.

"Oh, good," said his mother.

"Great," said his father again.

Alec smiled, anticipating his father's reaction to his next statement. "I got a basket," he announced proudly.

"Oh, good," said his mother.

Alec watched as his father chewed his mouthful of pizza. At last he swallowed and wiped his mouth with his napkin. "That's great, Alec," he said, biting off another hunk. "I'm really proud of you."

Alec stared. *I'm really proud of you?* That was it? No hooting and hollering? No jumping up and thumping him on the back? Not even a handshake?

Alec took a bite of his own pizza and chewed it slowly. It tasted like cardboard. He put the rest down.

"Can I be excused?" he asked.

"Something wrong, Alec?" his mother asked. "You usually eat more than that."

Alec shook his head. "I'm just not hungry. And I've got a lot of homework." He got up and grabbed his books off the counter. The photocopy of his missing report card fell out of his notebook.

"Oh, here," he said, picking it up and reluctantly holding it out to his father. "I got a copy of that report card that I lost."

Alec's father sat back in his chair and took the paper from Alec's hand. He opened it and frowned.

"Well, that's just great, Alec," he said. "What kind of money do you ever expect to make if you keep getting lousy grades like this?"

"Let me see," said Alec's mother. She took the paper and looked at it.

"They're not that bad," she said.

"He got a C — in math," Alec's father complained.

"Well, there's more to life than math," his mother said. "He got a B in English."

"Oh, great," said Alec's father. "Maybe he'll be a *poet.* Poets make lots of money, don't they?"

Alec's mother's eyes flashed. "Maybe he'll be a *lawyer*," she said. "Did you ever think of that?"

Alec's father didn't answer.

"I make just as much money as you do," Alec's mother went on.

Alec's father rolled his eyes up toward the ceiling. "I know, I know," he said. "You never let me forget. Look, I'm sorry if I offended you, okay? If Alec wants to be a lawyer, that's fine with me."

Alec's mother still didn't look satisfied, but she didn't argue any further. She looked back down at the paper.

"Alec," she said, "it says here your math teacher wants a parent conference. Why didn't you say something? Parent conferences are tonight."

Alec shrugged. "I didn't know," he said. "I never looked at my report card before I lost it on Friday."

Alec's mother frowned. She handed the paper back to Alec's father.

"Well, you'll have to go," she said. "I have too much work to do tonight."

Alec's father pushed the paper back across the table. "*I'm* not going," he argued. "I've got racquetball."

"Well, somebody's got to go," said Alec's mother.

Kelly got up from the table. "Don't look at me," she said. "He's not my kid." She walked out of the room.

Alec's mother smiled thinly. "John," she said, "you play racquetball every Monday. I have to get this brief written tonight. Can't you please go?"

Alec's father crossed his hands over his chest. "If you recall," he said tightly, "I didn't play last week. I went to college night at Kelly's school because *you* had to work late. Again."

Alec's parents stared at each other across the table in stony silence.

Alec swallowed. "Nobody has to go," he said weakly. "I'll just say you were both busy."

Alec's mother abruptly stood up, clutching the paper in her hand.

"Of course somebody has to go," she snapped, continuing to glare at Alec's father. "And of course it will be the mother, as usual."

Alec's father stood up, too. "Don't give me that martyr act," he said. "I do as much for these kids as you do."

"Oh, right." Alec's mother narrowed her eyes. "It's still a man's world," she snapped. "I don't care what anybody says."

Alec's father grabbed the paper from her hand. "Give me that," he snarled.

Alec's mother tried to grab the paper back, and it ripped in two.

"There," said Alec's father, throwing it to the floor. "Are you happy?" He turned and stalked out of the room.

"Where do you think you're going?" Alec's mother screeched.

"To the school, to talk about my son, the genius!"

The door slammed, and then Alec heard the Porsche squeal out of the driveway. He stood silent, staring at the floor.

His mother touched his arm.

"I'm sorry, Alec," she said. But she didn't sound sorry.

Her voice was still tense with anger. "I just don't under-stand your father sometimes. It seems like all he ever thinks of is himself."

Alec didn't answer. It wasn't like his mother to criticize his father behind his back. His parents had always had their fights, just like other married people, but they would never criticize each other to Alec or Kelly. It made Alec uncomfortable.

His mother sighed. "Would you mind if I went upstairs?" she asked. "I really need to get started."

Alec shook his head.

"Can you pick up the dishes?"

Alec nodded.

"Thanks, Pooh." His mother squeezed his arm affec-tionately, then went upstairs.

Tears filled Alec's eyes.

"I'm not Pooh," he whispered.

Alec's father wasn't home by the time his mother fin-ished. He still wasn't home by bedtime. Alec lay awake for a long time, listening for the return of the Porsche. His stomach ached, and his pillow grew damp from the tears that slowly filled his eyes and spilled down his cheeks. He was so confused. Everyone had changed. His mother, his father — even Kelly was aloof and uninter-ested in anything to do with the family. How could little Stevie have made such a difference? Somehow, not having had Stevie had changed his family in ways Alec couldn't understand.

Alec had to find a way to get Stevie back, for his family's sake, and for his own sake, too. God, he missed him. Alec took a deep breath, and the loneliness ached like a knife lodged up under his ribs. How could he have been so mean to Stevie? Sure, the kid was a pest sometimes. . . . Alec smiled sadly. The truth was, he was a pest most of the time, but as he looked back now, it was plain to see that a lot of the pestiness was just Stevie's way of trying to get close to Alec. Stevie had never cared if Alec stunk at sports or did lousy in school. Stevie had loved him, just for being Alec. And Alec had wished him away. . . .

The distant hum of an engine pierced Alec's concentration, and he crossed his fingers and prayed that the car would slow and turn into their driveway. It did, and Alec breathed a sigh of relief. He heard the garage door open and close, then listened to his father's footsteps trudging through the house and slowly up the stairs.

Alec longed to call out the way he used to when he was small and frightened by a nightmare. He longed for his father to come in and hold him tight and whisper, "It's all right. I'm here, Alec. It's all right."

Only now his father was a stranger. And nothing was all right.

Suddenly there was a deeper shadow in the darkness of the doorway. Alec closed his eyes quickly, pretending sleep. The floorboards creaked as the shadow moved closer, then stopped beside the bed. There was a long silence. Alec struggled to keep his breathing rhythmic and slow and to keep his eyelids from twitching. At last there was a weighty sigh, and Alec smelled a whiff of liquor as his father bent over him. A kiss brushed his forehead, followed by a barely perceptible whisper. "Goodnight, Pooh."

Alec swallowed hard and pressed his eyes tighter against the tears.

CHAPTER 18

Alec stood outside Meadowbrook High the next afternoon, watching the older kids stream out through the double front doors. He caught sight of Kelly and ducked behind a shrub until she passed. Then he stepped out onto the walk again. His mouth was dry, and he couldn't find a comfortable place to put his hands. Putting them in his pockets made him look too self-conscious, he thought, and crossing them over his chest, too cocky. But hanging them down made him look like an ape. He settled for one hand in a pocket and the other hanging down.

Then suddenly she was there. She was walking with a couple of girlfriends. They talked and laughed easily, unaware of Alec standing there in his private agony. He tried to call out as they walked by, but the words stuck in his throat. He stumbled along after them, trying to get up the nerve to speak. At last the two friends waved good-bye and stepped into a waiting car, and she was all alone. It was now or never.

"Abbey?" said Alec, his palms slick with perspiration now.

She turned and looked at him. Her expression was blank for a moment, but then flickered with recognition.

"Oh, hi," she said. "You're Kelly's brother, right?"

Alec nodded. "Alec Lansing," he confirmed.

"Hi, Alec," said Abbey. An amused smile played around her lips. "Did you come to tell me hi from Kelly again?"

Alec blushed. "No," he said. "I, uh, wondered if I could talk to you about something?"

Abbey shrugged. "I suppose so," she said. "What is it?"

"Well, you know how you said you were out at the mall last Friday?"

Abbey nodded.

"Well, did you by any chance see an old lady coming up the stairs?"

Alec crossed his fingers and prayed that his hunch was right. Even though things had changed for him, it seemed that Abbey and the old lady still would have been at the same place at the same time.

Abbey considered a moment, then nodded slowly.

"Was she carrying a big shopping bag?" she asked.

Alec nodded. "Yes! She was breathing heavily and coughing a lot, and she had a real hard time climbing the stairs."

Abbey nodded again. "Yeah," she said. "I saw her. I even offered her a ride home. She didn't look well to me."

Alec's excitement was growing. "Then you know where she lives?" he asked.

Abbey shook her head. "No," she said. "She didn't want a ride." Abbey's voice grew quiet. "I don't think she had a home to go to."

Alec's heart sank. "No home?" he said. "What do you mean?"

"I mean I think she was a street person. Why are you so interested in her?"

Alec felt like the carpet had been pulled out from under him. A street person? Where would he start to look for a street person? He fought back tears of disappointment.

"Alec?" Abbey broke into his thoughts again. "What's wrong? What's this all about?"

Alec looked at her. Her eyes were gentle and caring. He remembered her concern for the old woman, and he knew that she was sincere. He longed to tell her the truth, to share the awful burden he'd been carrying all alone these past few days, but he knew that was impossible. No one would ever believe him.

"I . . . I've got to find her," Alec said.

"But why?" Abbey asked.

"I . . . I have something that belongs to her. I think it may be valuable, and I want to give it back." It wasn't a lie. Oh, how he wished he *could* give it back.

Abbey looked skeptical. "How did you get something that belongs to her?" she asked.

"She gave it to me," said Alec, "for, uh, safekeeping."

Abbey smiled indulgently. "I wouldn't worry about it," she said. "In the first place, I don't think anything she had would really be valuable, and in the second place, she didn't seem to be thinking too clearly. She seemed a bit eccentric to me."

Reason was failing, and Alec was growing desperate. Tears were threatening to spill out of his eyes. "Look," he said, his voice trembling, "I've still got to find her. Did she say anything, anything at all, about where she was going?"

Abbey's smile faded. She shook her head slowly. "No, Alec," she said. "I'm sorry."

Alec couldn't hold back the tears any longer. He brushed them quickly off his cheeks and turned away. "Okay, thanks," he said over his shoulder. "I better go."

"Alec, wait." Abbey touched his arm. He wiped his eyes again and turned back to her.

"Look," she said, "I don't know what this is all about, but if it's that important to you, I have an idea where you can start to look."

A glimmer of hope pierced the darkness in Alec's heart. "Really, where?"

"There's a soup kitchen not far from the mall. I work there with my church group. I'll take you there if you like. Someone may know her."

Alec wanted to throw his arms around Abbey and hug her. "You'd do that?" he asked incredulously.

Abbey shrugged and smiled. "Sure," she said. "I don't have anything better to do today anyway."

CHAPTER 19

Alec sat in the front seat of Abbey's old station wagon, staring out the window.

"Are you always this quiet?" asked Abbey.

Alec felt himself blushing. He looked over at Abbey shyly. He wasn't used to being alone with girls, especially beautiful, older ones. He smiled awkwardly. "Not always," he said.

"How old are you, Alec?" asked Abbey.

"Thirteen."

Abbey raised her eyebrows. "Wow," she said. "You're tall for thirteen."

Alec blushed again. "Yeah."

"Must be a good basketball player, huh?" said Abbey.

Alec stiffened. "Okay, I guess."

Abbey looked over at him. Then she smiled.

"I bet you hate that, don't you?"

"What?" asked Alec.

"People assuming that you've got to be into basketball, just because you're tall."

Alec smiled. "Sort of."

Abbey laughed. "I know how it is," she said. "People are always assuming I want to be a model when I grow up, just because I look like one."

"Really?" said Alec. It was the first time he'd ever met anyone who felt the way he felt.

"Yeah," Abbey continued. "I think sometimes that if you're tall, or good-looking, or you have something else that makes you stand out, that's all people see. They don't take the time to find out what you're really like." She gave a little laugh. "I get mad, especially when boys treat me that way. I feel like yelling, 'Hey! There's a real person in here, not just a face and a body. Doesn't anybody care who *I* am?'"

Alec stared at her and his heart thumped in his chest. I care, Abbey, he wanted to whisper. I care a lot. Instead, he turned and stared out the window again.

They crossed the Meadowbrook town line into the city of Riverport, and the scenery shifted from neat, single-family houses to run-down old textile mills and dilapidated apartment buildings, from manicured yards to rubbish-strewn streets and alleys.

"That's it up ahead," said Abbey.

She eased the car over next to the curb in front of an old store front that had MISSION OF OUR LADY OF SORROWS painted across the window. Abbey looked at her watch. "Won't be too many customers yet," she said, "but maybe we can find one of the sisters."

Alec followed Abbey into the building. He stood for a moment in the doorway, letting his eyes adjust to the dimness after the glare of the sun and the snow outside. At last he could make out a row of rough-hewn tables running side by side the length of the room. An old man sat at one of them. In a corner, a forlorn little Christmas tree blinked off and on. At the far end of the room a window was cut into the wall, and beyond the window two women stood with their backs to him, preparing food. Abbey walked over to the window. Alec followed.

"Excuse me," said Abbey.

The women turned around and looked at her.

"I wonder if you could help us?" Abbey went on. "We're looking for someone."

They stared at her blankly. Then one of them shrugged and shook her head apologetically. "*No hablo inglés*," she said.

Abbey nodded. "*Está aquí Sor Barbara?*" she asked.

The women broke into smiles and pointed to a door off to one side of the kitchen.

"*Muchas gracias*," said Abbey. She turned to Alec. "Sister Barbara is upstairs in her apartment," she told him. "I'll run up and get her." She lifted a section at one end of the counter, then crossed the kitchen and disappeared through the door.

Left alone, Alec turned and looked around the room again. The old man seated at the table was disheveled and unkempt, with a gray stubble of beard. He ignored Alec and stared down at his bowl of soup. Alec watched as he tried to raise the spoon to his lips. His hand shook so badly that the soup spilled off the spoon before it ever got to his mouth. He tried again and again, with no success. At last he put the spoon down and stared off into space, tears of frustration rimming his eyes.

Alec's heart went out to the man. He walked over and sat down beside him.

"Here," he said, lifting the spoon, "let me give you a hand." The man turned red, watery eyes to him. He seemed surprised by Alec's offer, and Alec thought for a moment that he might refuse help, but at last he opened his mouth and allowed himself to be fed.

The front door opened, and a woman with two young children came in. Alec stared at them, surprised at how clean and neatly dressed they were. The woman seemed embarrassed by Alec's stare, so he looked away as she made her way up to the food window.

Before long there were footsteps on the back stairs, and a cheerful-looking woman in a red dress bustled ahead of Abbey into the kitchen. She lifted the section of counter, nodded pleasantly to the young mother, and she and Abbey came out into the room. The sister had curly silver hair and a bright smile. Only the large cross that hung around her neck gave a clue that she was a nun. She smiled down at Alec.

"Sister Barbara," said Abbey, "I'd like you to meet my friend, Alec Lansing."

"Hello, Alec," said the nun. "Aren't you good to help Raymond. How are you today, Raymond?" She put an arm around the old man's shoulders and gave him a warm hug. He smiled shyly and nodded his appreciation.

Sister Barbara patted Alec on the back and took the spoon from his hand. "I'll take over now, thank you," she said. "What can I do for you two young people?"

Alec slid down the bench to make room for the sister.

"We're looking for someone," said Abbey. "We wondered if you might have seen her."

"Oh?" said Sister Barbara. "What's her name?"

Abbey turned to Alec and Alec blushed. "I . . . I don't know," he said, "but she was dressed kind of in rags, and she carried this big shopping bag."

Sister Barbara smiled sadly. "That description would fit many of the women that come in here," she said. "Can't you tell me anything more?"

Alec thought. "She wore a flowered scarf on her head that was all faded, but that looked like it used to be brightly colored," he said, "and she spoke strangely."

"Strangely how?" Sister Barbara asked.

"I don't know," said Alec. "Just . . . not like you'd expect an old woman like her to sound. Musical, sort of."

The sister shook her head slowly. "I'm sorry," she said. "No one comes to mind. Why are you looking for her?"

"I have something that belongs to her," said Alec, "and I'd like to give it back."

Sister Barbara sighed. "Well," she said, "I wish I could be of more help. Why don't you try Saint Patrick's shelter on the other side of town?" She raised another spoon of soup to the old man's lips. He shook his head and pushed it away.

"Gypsy," he said softly.

Sister Barbara turned to him.

"What did you say, Raymond?" she asked.

The old man looked up at them all timidly, as if it frightened him to have to speak. "We call her Gypsy," he said, barely above a whisper.

"You know the woman they're looking for?" the sister prompted.

Raymond nodded and licked his dry, cracked lips. "She lives over on Fulton Street."

"Do you know what address?" Alec asked eagerly.

The man seemed confused.

"Fulton Street," he repeated.

"But —" Alec began to ask again, when Sister Barbara put a hand on his arm.

"I think," she said, "that Raymond means this woman lives *on* the street, not in a house on the street."

Raymond nodded, and Alec felt his face flush with embarrassment.

"Oh," he said quietly.

"Come on," Abbey said to Alec. "We'll take a drive over there. It's not far."

Alec nodded, and Sister Barbara walked them to the door. A young man was just coming in. He had a suit on, and Abbey seemed to know him well.

"Hi, Nick," she said. "Any luck yet?"

The man shook his head tiredly. "Not yet," he said. "But I'm not giving up."

"Good for you," said Abbey.

Nick nodded to them all, then made his way up to the window.

Sister Barbara turned her attention back to Alec and Abbey. "Good luck," she said.

They each thanked her in turn. Then Alec turned back. "Good-bye, Raymond," he called. "I appreciate your help."

The old man waved with a badly trembling hand.

"Is he going to be all right?" Alec whispered to Sister Barbara.

The sister shook her head. "He has problems with alcohol," she said.

"Alcohol?" said Alec. "Then, shouldn't he be in some kind of treatment center?"

"Treatment centers for people like Raymond are too few and too full," the sister said softly. "Here we feel fortunate if we have food enough to feed their bellies and love enough to feed their souls."

CHAPTER 20

Alec was quiet and thoughtful as Abbey steered the car through the crowded, downtown business district. "You know something funny?" he said at last. "Those people in there, they weren't all like Raymond and Gypsy."

Abbey arched an eyebrow. "How do you mean?" she asked.

"Well, like, some of them were clean and neat. That guy Nick, for instance. He didn't look like a bum or anything."

Abbey glanced at Alec sharply, and there was a note of irritation in her voice when she spoke. "Not everyone who's hungry is a bum, Alec. Anybody can lose a job or have a streak of bad luck."

Alec flushed with embarrassment. "Sorry," he mumbled.

Abbey's expression softened somewhat. "That's okay," she said. "It's not your fault."

They parked in the Fulton Street parking garage, then went down in the elevator and out onto the street.

"Now what?" asked Alec.

"I guess we just walk around and look for her," Abbey said with a shrug.

Fulton Street was lined with tall office buildings and expensive shops, all gaily trimmed for Christmas. Men in suits and overcoats hurried along, carrying attaché cases and glancing at their watches. Well-dressed women did the same, their high-heeled boots clicking impatiently along the sidewalk. Other, equally well-dressed women strolled at a more leisurely pace, stopping to scrutinize displays in the shop windows. Here and there small children were tugged along or pushed in strollers, whining with boredom and fatigue. Where in this affluent maze, Alec wondered, would someone like Gypsy live?

"Look," said Abbey. She nodded toward the other side of the street. "Maybe those guys might know her."

Before Alec could answer, Abbey was on her way across the street. Alec followed. The guys Abbey had referred to were two men who sat huddled against the side of the Federal Savings Bank, warming their feet over a steaming grate in the sidewalk. They were shabbily dressed. The younger of the two had long, greasy hair, wrapped with a dirty headband. He wore an old Army jacket, and the left sleeve appeared to be flat and empty. No hand protruded from the end. In his right hand, the man held a cigarette. His eyes were closed, and he hummed tunelessly to himself, pausing now and then to take a deep drag on the cigarette.

The other, older, man was slouched down with his legs sprawled across the grate. Alec noted uncomfortably that the man's fly was open, and the man didn't seem to know or care. His pants were a dirty, greasy green. He had a knit cap pulled low over his eyes and was wearing a worn red-checked hunting jacket over several layers of grungy sweaters. He stared with glazed eyes at passersby.

"Excuse me," Abbey said to the younger man. He went on nodding to his garbled tune.

"Excuse me," Abbey said, louder this time. The old man in the cap swung his eyes slowly in her direction.

"Whad'ya want?" he barked.

"I . . . was just going to ask your friend a question," said Abbey.

"He don't hear nothin'," said the man. The younger man went right on nodding.

"Oh," said Abbey, "I'm sorry. Maybe you could help us then. We're looking for someone."

The man's eyes narrowed suspiciously, and he turned away, ignoring the question.

"Her name is Gypsy," Alec put in. "She's a . . . friend."

The man swung his eyes up toward Alec. "Ain't no gypsies around here," he mumbled.

"No," said Alec, "I said her name —"

The man looked away again, and Abbey put her hand on Alec's arm.

"Come on," she said. "We'll just keep looking."

They walked a little farther.

Just ahead, a heavyset man in a ragged overcoat came

out of one of the department stores. He walked up the street and turned into an alley. When Abbey and Alec caught up with him, he was leaning against the wall with his back to them. He had taken off one shoe, and was peeling black, tarlike strips of what must have been a sock from a foot that was equally black underneath. As Alec and Abbey watched, he produced a new pair of socks from under the folds of his coat and proceeded to pull one on.

"Come on," Abbey whispered. "I don't want him to think we're spying."

"Do you think he just stole those socks?" Alec asked as they headed down the street again.

Abbey shrugged. "Maybe," she said. "Maybe he just begged them from someone."

Alec swallowed hard, wondering how it must feel to be desperate enough to beg for a pair of socks. He thought guiltily of the dozens of mismatched pairs that cluttered his drawers at home.

They had reached another alley. A young girl lounged by the entrance.

"Amber!" Abbey called out.

The girl turned quickly to look at her. She was small and thin, and dressed very scantily for the weather. She seemed to recognize Abbey, too.

"Hello," she said, staring shyly down at the sidewalk as Alec and Abbey approached. She didn't look to Alec like she could be much older than he was, although she wore a lot of makeup.

"How are you?" asked Abbey.

The girl nodded to indicate that she was okay, but she rubbed her arms briskly and trembled with the cold.

"I haven't seen you at the shelter in a while," said Abbey.

"No," said the girl softly. "I been . . . workin'. I got me a place to stay now."

"Oh," said Abbey quietly.

The girl looked down again and fidgeted uneasily.

"Well, if you need anything," said Abbey, "you know where we are."

The girl nodded without looking up. Alec touched Abbey's arm and mouthed the name Gypsy.

"Oh, right," said Abbey. "Amber, would you happen to know of an old woman who lives around here? They call her Gypsy?"

Amber looked up again and nodded slowly. "Yeah," she said, "I know her. She been sleeping under the stairs in the alley behind the Ship's Wheel Café."

"Under the stairs?" Alec repeated.

Amber glanced at him. "Yeah," she said. "Why?"

"I, uh, nothing," Alec stammered. "Just . . . how could anyone sleep under a stairway?"

Amber shrugged. "It's as good a place as any," she said. "She ain't there no more, though. Ambulance took her yesterday."

"Ambulance?" Alec gasped.

"Yeah." Amber shook her head. "She was pretty sick. I don't guess she'll be back."

A police car drove by slowly, and Amber grew uneasy. "I gotta go," she said, hurrying off up the street in the opposite direction.

"Wait!" shouted Alec. "Do you know where the ambulance took her?"

Amber laughed. "City Hospital," she said. "That's where all us charity cases go."

"Good-bye, Amber," Abbey called out. "Good luck."

"I wonder why that cop car made her so nervous," Alec said.

Abbey shook her head slowly. "I don't know," she said. "I've got a few ideas. I just hope they're wrong."

"What do you mean?" asked Alec.

Abbey looked up at him and smiled sadly. "You've led a pretty sheltered life, haven't you?" she said.

Alec shrugged apologetically. "I . . . I dunno," he said. "I guess so."

Abbey nodded. "You don't have to feel bad about it," she said. "Most of the kids in Meadowbrook don't know about these things. Their parents would prefer they never saw this side of life. So would mine, to tell the truth."

Alec looked back up the street in the direction they had come from. An old woman was picking through a trash can near the corner. Alec saw her take out a rumpled piece of paper, unwrap it, and stuff whatever was inside it into her mouth. His stomach turned over. "They're everywhere," he said quietly. Then he looked at Abbey and added remorsefully, "And I've never seen them before. I've been to this city so many times, and I've never really seen them."

"It's all right," said Abbey. "Not many people do."

Suddenly Alec grew angry, angry at everything he had seen and angry at Abbey for treating him like some naive little kid who was too young to care.

"No," he said sharply. "It's *not* all right. Stop pretending that it is."

Abbey's eyes widened at his response. "Okay," she said.

They started walking back toward the garage.

"So what are you going to do about it?" Abbey challenged.

"What?"

"If it's not okay, what are *you* going to do about it?"

Alec swallowed uncomfortably. "Me?"

"Yeah, you?"

Alec stared down at his feet. He would like to do something about it. He really would. But what?

"We can always use an extra pair of hands down at the shelter," Abbey prompted.

Alec looked up. "Really?"

"Sure," said Abbey. "You could ride with me. I work every Monday after school."

Alec started to smile. He liked the idea of being able to work at the shelter. He enjoyed helping people. It always gave him a good feeling inside. And spending every Monday with Abbey didn't sound too bad either. Then he remembered something, and his smile faded.

"Mondays?" he said dejectedly. "I've got a basketball game every Monday."

Abbey looked confused. "I thought you said you didn't play basketball."

"I said I didn't like it. I didn't say I didn't play it."

Abbey shook her head. "I don't get it," she said. "Why do you play it if you don't like it?"

Alec sighed. "It's a long story."

Abbey laughed. They had reached the garage and were on the way up to the car. "So tell me on the way home," she said.

"Home?" said Alec. "What do you mean home? Aren't we going to the hospital?"

"The hospital?"

"Yeah. To find Gypsy."

Abbey looked doubtful. "Oh, I don't know, Alec. It's getting late, and Amber seemed to think —"

"Please," said Alec. "The hospital isn't far, and it won't take me long. I've got to try."

Abbey smiled and sighed tiredly. "Okay," she said, "but this is the last stop."

"Absolutely," said Alec. "I promise. You're the best."

CHAPTER 21

"So?" said Abbey as she guided the station wagon out of the parking garage.

"So what?" asked Alec.

"So, what's your long story?"

"Oh." Alec laughed. "It's not that long really. It's just that my dad is really into sports, and . . ." Alec got a sinking feeling in his chest and couldn't go on. At least he *was,* he added silently, before . . .

"I know," Abbey continued. "The same old story. Sports fan father makes son play, whether he likes it or not, because it's *good* for him. Team play builds character. Sports are great preparation for life. Rah, rah, rah!"

Alec smiled in spite of himself. "Yeah," he said. "Something like that."

"Have you told him how you really feel?" Abbey asked.

Alec thought back to his old father and shook his head. "No," he said. "He wouldn't understand."

"Do me a favor and try it sometime," said Abbey. "Parents aren't as bad as you think. They really do want us to be happy, you know. I found that out when I butted heads with my parents over working at the shelter."

"You fight with your parents?" said Alec.

"Of course." Abbey grinned. "Doesn't everybody? Parents seem to think that because something worked for them, it should work for us. My folks thought I should spend my extracurricular time being a cheerleader. A cheerleader! Can you imagine?"

Alec smiled. He could imagine. Very well, actually. Abbey looked like the epitome of a cheerleader, but he decided he'd better not say so. Instead he shook his head sympathetically and said, "*Un*believable."

Abbey nodded. "Yeah," she said. Then she smiled. "But they were really just concerned. When they found out how important working at the shelter was to me, they came around. Do me a favor and try talking to your dad. He might surprise you."

Alec shrugged. "Okay," he said quietly. Somehow he doubted it would be much of an issue anymore. He was beginning to realize that having parents who were concerned about you, even *overly* concerned, wasn't the worst thing in the world.

"Something wrong?" asked Abbey after a while. They were approaching the hospital.

"No," said Alec. "It's just that . . . I hate hospitals."

It was the truth. He could feel his insides tightening up as soon as they pulled into the parking lot. They walked up a steep hill to the main entrance. A guard stood just inside the front doors, and Alec glanced at him warily, wondering if it was his job to keep people out or to keep people in.

Abbey was already at the reception desk, and Alec hurried to catch up with her.

"We're looking for an old woman who was just brought in yesterday," she said. "She goes by the name of Gypsy."

"Gypsy who?" asked the receptionist.

"Just Gypsy," said Alec.

The woman frowned but began to punch the keys on her computer. "No one by that name here," she said.

Alec looked dejectedly at Abbey.

"She must be," Abbey told the woman. "She's a . . . kind of a bag lady."

The woman's frown deepened. She punched some more keys and stared at the screen. "Transient, female, age approximately seventy, identity unknown," she read out.

"That's her," said Alec. "I'm sure that's her."

The woman nodded. "I'm afraid you can't go up," she said. "She's in intensive care. Only immediate family can visit."

Alec swallowed and gave Abbey a quick glance. "We're her grandchildren," he said.

The receptionist eyed him suspiciously. "You don't look like the grandchildren of a bag lady," she answered.

Alec could feel his ears starting to burn the way they did whenever he tried to lie. "Our, uh, father disowned her," he said, "because she was an alcoholic, but we still care about her, and we'd like to see her. It's really important to us."

The woman looked unconvinced, but at last she handed them a yellow pass. "Take the elevator to the fifth floor, and follow the red stripe on the wall," she said.

Alec smiled. "Thanks," he told her.

Abbey rolled her eyes at him in the elevator. "Grandchildren?" she said.

Alec shrugged and grinned. He and Abbey got off on the fifth floor and followed the red stripe through a pair of swinging doors. On the other side was a huge room divided all around the outside into a bunch of little cubicles, with a big nurse's station in the center.

Each cubicle had a patient in it, and the patients were hooked up to all kinds of wires and machines and tubes. It was scary. Alec wanted to turn and run before somebody stuck a tube into him by mistake, but Abbey walked calmly up to the nurse's station.

"We're here to see our grandmother," she said, handing the nurse the pass.

The nurse looked at the number on the pass, then looked at Abbey and Alec. She arched an eyebrow. "She's your grandmother?" she said.

Abbey nodded convincingly. "How is she doing?" she asked.

The nurse's attitude softened. "Not well," she said. "She's refused any life support. It's just a matter of time." She nodded over her shoulder. "She's in thirty-two."

Abbey nodded solemnly, then gestured to Alec. Alec swallowed his fear and followed her to one of the little cubicles. They stepped inside.

The woman on the bed was barely recognizable as the woman they had met at the mall. Her skin was white, and her straight, gray hair spilled out around her on the pillow. Without all her clothes and coats on, she seemed far less bulky under the sheets. Her head was back and her mouth open. She breathed in loud, raspy spurts, and an ominous gurgle sounded in her throat. Wires ran from her chest to a little television screen on which a bright green dot bounced up and down rhythmically.

Alec had never been close to a critically ill person before, and he was frightened. He hung back by the door until Abbey pushed him forward.

"Talk to her," she whispered. "There may not be much time."

Alec walked over to the bed. He could feel himself trembling.

"Gypsy?" he said hoarsely.

The eyelids flickered, and the startling blue eyes stared out of the pale face. Alec saw instant recognition in them.

"Alec?" the woman said in her soft, fluid voice.

Alec nodded. "How do you know my name?" he asked, surprised.

She smiled tiredly. "I have a good memory," she answered. Her face suddenly screwed up, and she went off into a terrible fit of coughing. In the midst of it, a sharply dressed woman stepped into the room. She paid no attention to the hacking old woman, but turned to Alec and Abbey instead.

"I'm Mrs. Donovan," she said brightly. "I understand that you are the grandchildren of this patient?"

Alec and Abbey exchanged glances, then nodded unsurely.

Mrs. Donovan smiled. "In that case," she said, "I'd like to talk to you about the bill."

"The . . . the bill?" Alec stammered. The old woman went off into another fit of coughing, and Alec glanced at her fearfully. He felt a hand on his arm and turned to find Abbey standing beside him.

"You keep Granny company, Alec," she said with a secretive wink. "I'll talk to Mrs. Donovan out in the hall."

Alec nodded his appreciation, then turned quickly back to the old woman. "Gypsy," he whispered again, as soon as the coughing stopped.

She shook her head slowly. "My name is not Gypsy," she said. "It is Yohilda."

Alec stared at her. "Who are you?" he asked. "Where are you from?"

The old woman smiled tremulously. "From everywhere, and nowhere. I am a Wanderer."

Alec frowned. He had no time for double talk. "But . . . you . . . you're some kind of magic," he said.

The woman nodded. "You could call it that."

Alec shook his head. "It doesn't make sense," he said. "If you really are magic, why do you live like you do?"

"It is a Wanderer's lot to live on the kindness of others, rewarding that kindness wherever . . . ag . . . agh . . ."

The old woman gagged and started to cough again. Alec looked nervously around the small steel-and-glass cubicle, trying to absorb the woman's strange words and wondering once again if he could be dreaming.

The woman's coughing slowed, and she dabbed at her eyes with a corner of the bedsheet. She sighed heavily. "I will not be sorry to leave your world," she rasped. "Your world is not . . . kind . . . to strangers."

"*My* world? *Leave?*" Fear suddenly gripped Alec's heart. "But the talisman," he said quickly. "You've got to take it back."

The old woman looked surprised. "You don't . . . want it?" she said. She began to cough again.

Alec shook his head emphatically.

The woman held out a trembling hand. "All right then," she gasped, fighting for breath. "Give it to me."

"I don't have it," said Alec.

"Where . . . where . . . is it then?" The old woman seemed to be choking on every word.

"I used it," said Alec. "I —" He could hardly bring himself to utter the words. "I wished my brother had never been born."

The old woman's head sank back into the pillow. She closed her eyes, and Alec saw a tear squeeze out of the corner of one.

"I didn't mean it," Alec rushed on. "I never dreamed it would work. You've got to help me get him back!"

The old woman lay still.

"Yohilda!" Alec shook her arm. "Yohilda, please!"

Yohilda's eyes fluttered open. They were filled with a great sadness. "I'm s-sorry," she whispered. "There is nothing I can do." She closed her eyes again.

"Nothing you can do!" Alec's heart raced. "There must be. There has to be. Nobody believes me. Nobody remembers. You have to help me."

Yohilda's chest rose with a raspy intake of breath. "In time," she said, "you will forget, too."

"Forget? I don't want to forget. I want my brother back."

A great tremor shook Yohilda's body, and the little green dot on the television set began bouncing erratically. A nurse suddenly rushed into the room.

"I'm sorry," she said. "You'll have to leave."

"But —"

Two more nurses rushed in and pushed Alec aside. He stepped back, his heart thumping, as they drew a big green curtain around the bed.

CHAPTER 22

Alec staggered out into the fluorescent white glare of the hall. A young doctor rushed by him into the room.

"Alec?" Abbey disengaged herself from Mrs. Donovan and hurried over. "Alec, are you okay? You look awful."

"I think —" Alec stammered. "I think she's dying."

They both turned to look back through the window of the cubicle. There was a flurry of activity behind the curtain, and then, after a few minutes, everything grew quiet. Two of the nurses came back out. One walked over to them.

"I'm sorry," she said. Alec swallowed hard and stared down at the floor. He felt a gentle touch on his arm and looked up again into Abbey's sympathetic eyes.

"Come on," she said softly. "I'll buy you a soda."

They walked in silence down to the coffee shop. Abbey bought a cup of coffee for herself and a Coke for Alec. He sat down and stared at it, stirring the ice around mindlessly with his straw.

"Pretty awful, isn't it?" said Abbey.

Alec nodded.

"Have you ever seen anyone die before?"

Alec shook his head slowly. "I didn't even say goodbye to her," he said. "Nobody said good-bye to her."

Abbey reached across the table and squeezed his arm. "You didn't know," she said.

"I was just thinking about my problem," said Alec. "And there she was . . . dying."

Abbey looked puzzled. "Your problem?" she asked. "What do you mean, your problem?"

Alec swallowed. "Nothing," he said. *Nothing*. The word echoed in the hollows of his heart. *Nothing I can do.* And now Yohilda was gone, and with her all hope of ever getting Stevie back. For the first time, the full realization of what he had done swept over him.

"My God," he whispered. Sweat broke out on his upper lip, and his body began to shake.

Abbey jumped up, alarmed. She came over to Alec's side of the table and wrapped her arms around him comfortingly. "It's okay," she whispered. "It's okay."

Abbey's embrace loosed a momentary flood of tears from Alec's eyes. He brushed them away, aware that people were looking, and struggled to regain composure.

"I'm all right," he whispered hoarsely.

"Are you sure?" Abbey straightened and gave him a worried look.

Alec nodded and glanced awkwardly around the coffee shop. He took a deep drink of his Coke. Abbey sat back down and continued to stare at him with a troubled expression.

"Alec?" she said after a while. "*Was* she your grandmother? You can tell me the truth."

You can tell me the truth. Alec looked into Abbey's gentle, caring eyes and was tempted for a moment to blurt everything out. But then he stared back down at the table. This was the real world. The world of ice that clinked when you stirred it and cups that smelled like wax, of Formica tabletops with cigarette burns and salt-shakers smudged with ketchup. People didn't disappear in this world. Things weren't here one minute, gone the next. Alec would never be able to share his secret. Never. Unless he wanted to spend the rest of his life in an insane asylum.

"Can we go now?" he asked quietly.

"Sure," said Abbey.

They took the elevator back down to the first floor and handed their passes in to the receptionist. They started to walk away, when suddenly Alec turned back.

"Her name is Yohilda," he told the receptionist.

The woman looked at him strangely.

"The old woman," Alec went on. "The one you have listed as a transient. She has a name. It's Yohilda."

The woman nodded politely. "That's nice," she said.

"Would you write it in her file, please?" said Alec.

The woman frowned, but she tapped away on her computer keys. Alec leaned over her shoulder and watched as the file came up on her screen. In the top left corner, after the word NAME, the woman typed YOHILDA.

"Thank you," said Alec. Then he turned away.

Abbey was holding the door for him. She had a bemused smile on her lips. "You're a funny kid, Alec," she said. But the way she said it wasn't bad.

Alec shrugged tiredly. "No one should die without a name," he said.

They walked back down the hill to where the car was parked, slipping on the sidewalk salt and sand that rolled beneath their shoes. It was getting dark, and the lights were coming on in the city below.

"Pretty tree this year," said Abbey. She nodded toward the green, where a giant lighted Christmas tree stood. The sight of it deepened the ache in Alec's heart. It reminded him of his family's annual trip into Riverport to start their Christmas shopping and watch the tree-lighting ceremony. This year Stevie had blown all the money he had on a fishing knife for Alec. Alec knew because he'd overheard his mother trying to talk Stevie out of it.

"I don't care if I won't have any money to buy any other presents," Stevie had argued. "I'll make everybody else something. I saw Alec looking at this knife. He said it was *awesome*. I *have* to buy it for him. *Please?*"

Alec thought back to the fishing trips he and Stevie used to take together. Stevie was always so thrilled to be allowed to come along. He'd imitate every move Alec made, as if Alec were the source of all knowledge. It had never mattered to Stevie in the least that Alec couldn't catch anything bigger than a sunfish.

A small crowd of shoppers crisscrossed through the green. As Alec and Abbey drew closer, Alec noticed a little boy standing apart, staring up at the tree. A little boy with sandy hair and a green ski coat!

"Stevie!" Alec shouted. He sprinted across the street and ran up behind the little boy. The child turned and looked at him.

"Mommy!" he cried, bolting past Alec. A tall woman in a long red coat held a hand out to the child and stared at Alec suspiciously.

"*Alec?*"

Alec turned. He had forgotten Abbey. She stood watching him now.

"What was that all about?" she asked.

Alec stared down at the white ground, wondering if the ache in his stomach would ever go away again.

"Nothing," he said quietly. "I just thought I saw . . . an old friend."

CHAPTER 23

Alec knew nobody would be home yet, and he couldn't face the empty house, so he asked Abbey to drop him at Muzzy's.

"You sure you're all right now?" Abbey asked when they pulled into the driveway.

Alec nodded. "Yeah, thanks. And thanks for all your help."

"Anytime," said Abbey. Then she kind of shook her head a little and smiled a funny smile.

"What is it?" asked Alec.

"Nothing," said Abbey with a sigh. "It's just that . . . I sure wish you were a few years older."

"Why?" asked Alec, staring at her in confusion.

Abbey smiled wider. "Because you're the nicest guy I've ever met."

Alec felt a deep flush creep up his neck to his face. "I am?" he said, his brow crinkled up in disbelief.

Abbey laughed. "Yes," she said. "And that's precisely why — because you don't know it." She reached over and gave his hand an affectionate squeeze. "Do me a favor, Alec," she said. "Try not to change. Someday, three years won't seem like such a big difference."

"Sh-sure," Alec stammered. "I'll try." He got out of the car and stood staring in astonishment as Abbey backed out of Muzzy's driveway and blew him a farewell kiss. He staggered up Muzzy's walk with his head still whirling and rang the bell.

"Hey, worm poop!" someone yelled.

Alec looked down at Charlene, the older of Muzzy's two little sisters.

"It's about time," she complained. "I been standing here with the door open for five minutes. What do you want?"

"Is Muzzy home yet?" Alec asked.

Charlene shook her head. "Nope."

"Mind if I come in and wait?"

Charlene shook her head again. "Nope," she repeated. "We're putting up our Christmas tree!" She flung the door wide, then scooted down the hall and disappeared. Alec threw his coat over the others that were piled in the corner, then climbed over a mine field of wet boots and smelly sneakers into the kitchen. He lifted the lid of the bread box, grabbed a muffin to try and calm his queasy stomach, and followed the sounds of clamor and confusion into the family room. The easy informality of Muzzy's house comforted him.

"Alec," cried Muzzy's mother when he walked into the

room. "Just in time!" She was standing on a chair in the middle of a crowd of kids, leaning precariously in toward the Christmas tree. She held the treetop star in her outstretched hand.

Alec went over and took the star, then reached up and perched it neatly on the top of the tree.

"My hero," said Muzzy's mom, clasping her hands together and fluttering her lashes comically at Alec.

Alec grinned. Muzzy's mom always *could* make him smile.

"Okay, troops." She jumped down off the chair. "It's all yours."

Muzzy's little sisters and a horde of their friends began to attack the tree from every side. Ornaments flew in all directions. Mrs. Franklin waded through the crowd and stood beside Alec, shaking her head good-naturedly at all the confusion.

"Mrs. Franklin," said Alec suddenly, "would you mind if I asked you something?"

Mrs. Franklin shook her head. "Of course not, honey. What's on your mind?"

"Well, just . . . whatever made you decide to have Charlene and Rosie?"

Muzzy's mom gave Alec a startled glance, then threw her head back and laughed. "You can't figure it out either, huh?" she said.

Alec smiled. "No, I'm serious," he said. "I'm, uh, writing an essay on families."

"Oh, I see." Mrs. Franklin laughed again. "Well, actually that's an easy one. I just loved my little Muzzy so much, I couldn't imagine not having any more little babies after him."

Now it was Alec's turn to laugh. "No, Mrs. Franklin," he said again, "I really am serious."

Muzzy's mom smiled up at him, her eyes glowing with genuine warmth. "So am I, honey," she said.

Alec stared down at her. A little prickle ran up his spine, and suddenly he couldn't hold his lips in a smile anymore. *Because they loved him so much?* His parents had had Stevie because they had loved *Alec* so much?

Mrs. Franklin seemed to take Alec's reaction as a sign that she had offended him.

"Now, that's not to say that your mama doesn't love you," she added hurriedly. "For some folks, one child is plenty. For others, ten is not enough. The number doesn't matter. What matters is that folks follow their own hearts."

Alec nodded slowly, then turned and stared at the Christmas tree. His eyes misted over, and for a moment all the lights blurred together into a kaleidoscope of colors. At last he understood. His parents *had* followed their own hearts. But his wish had changed all that. It had changed who they were, and how they thought, and what they wanted out of life, and that's why Stevie had never been born.

The door from the garage into the family room suddenly flew open, and Muzzy stomped in in his hockey uniform. He frowned when he saw the crowd. "Jeez, Ma," he yelled. "Look at the mess they're making. I thought you were gonna wait for me."

Mrs. Franklin threw up her hands. "They took me hostage and tortured me, honey," she said. "I couldn't hold out any longer."

"What about Dad and Jim?"

"Jim's coach called an emergency practice. They just left." Mrs. Franklin gave Alec a baleful look. "Aren't you glad it isn't this crazy at your house?" she asked.

Alec smiled sadly but didn't answer.

"Why don't you two pitch in and give the little ones a hand?" Mrs. Franklin suggested. "I'll go whip up a batch of popcorn." She gave Muzzy an affectionate peck on the cheek on her way out to the kitchen.

"Come on, Giraffeman," said Muzzy. "We'd better take charge here." He pulled a box of ornaments away from nine-year-old Charlene.

"Hey," she yelled. "Give those back."

"No," Muzzy told her. "You're doing it all wrong. These go up on top." He handed the box to Alec and pointed toward the upper branches. Alec started hanging the ornaments. Charlene stuck her tongue out at him.

Muzzy pushed his other sister, five-year-old Rosie, out of the way and started pulling all her ornaments back off the tree.

"Hey," Rosie yelled. "You stop that. I want them there."

"Muzzy," called Mrs. Franklin from the kitchen, "you stop tormenting those children."

Muzzy went right on pulling ornaments off. "We can't leave these ornaments here, Ma," he yelled back. "Rosie's got ten on one branch. The whole tree's gonna fall over, she's got so much stuff on one side."

"I like it like that," Rosie whined. She grabbed one of the ornaments back from Muzzy, and it fell to the floor and smashed.

"Now look what you did, you little butt head," said Muzzy. He ran over and took a small box of ornaments out of the carton. "Here," he told Rosie. "These are for you."

Rosie held up the box of tiny, faded plastic ornaments. "These are for babies," she protested.

"That's right," said Muzzy, "and that's just what you are, a baby, so shut your mouth and hang 'em on the tree."

Alec looked at Rosie, who was staring forlornly at the ugly, unbreakable ornaments.

"Cool it, Muzz," he said. "Let her hang the nice ones." He handed his own box back to Charlene. "Here," he said. "Put them where you want them."

Muzzy stared at Alec as if he'd suddenly grown three horns and fangs. "What's got into you, man?" he asked.

Alec shook his head. "They're just little kids," he said. "Who cares what the tree looks like? Let them have fun."

Muzzy rolled his eyes. "Well, *pardon* me," he said, crossing his arms in front of his chest. "That's easy for you to say. You don't have to put up with any little rodents ruining your Christmas tree."

Alec left the bedlam of Muzzy's house behind and walked home in the quiet darkness. The snow crunched underfoot, and the stars twinkled brightly overhead. A blue-white sliver of moon hung in the sky. Where was Stevie? Alec wondered. Up there somewhere? And who had sent Yohilda? Was she an angel of some sort? Alec had always said his prayers and gone to church with his family, but he'd never thought much about God. He'd just kind of taken God for granted. For the first time, Alec tried to picture God as real, some kind of great, all-knowing being who stared back down at him now. Alec shivered. He didn't imagine God was too pleased.

"Your world is not kind to strangers," Yohilda had said. Alec thought about all the people he had seen on the street today. Then he thought about Muzzy's family, and his own, and about Stevie. "Kind to strangers?" he whispered sadly. "We aren't even kind to the people we love."

CHAPTER 24

Alec's street was all aglow. Holiday lights winked from every house, except his own. His house was dark and still. Only a pale blue-white glow in the family room window gave a sign that someone was home, watching TV.

Alec walked in and kicked his snowy shoes off in the back hall. He found Kelly sprawled on the family room floor watching reruns of *The Brady Bunch*.

"Hi," said Alec.

Kelly grunted in return.

"Where're Mom and Dad?"

"Mom called to say she wouldn't be home until nine, so Dad went to the club."

"What about dinner?"

Kelly held up a half eaten peanut-butter sandwich. "Make your own," she said.

Alec walked out into the kitchen and switched on the light. He slapped a peanut-butter sandwich together and took a bite, but it just stuck in his throat. He threw the rest into the sink and went up to put some old clothes on. He pulled his sweater off over his head, rolled it into a ball, and tossed it up on top of his closet. He was about to slide the closet door shut again when a white shape far back in the corner caught his eye. He reached back and took it down. It was Cupcake the Bear.

Tears welled up in Alec's eyes. He sat down on his bed and hugged the old bear tight.

"You miss him, too, don't you?" he whispered.

He held the bear out and looked at it through tear-blurred eyes. Its fur was thick with dust. Alec brushed it off gently. "You remember him, don't you, Cupcake?" he said, happy to have someone to talk to about Stevie at last, even if it was just a stuffed animal.

"I never knew how much I loved him," he went on. "I blamed him for all the trouble between me and Dad. But you know what? Stevie had nothing to do with that. Dad and I just got into a bad habit of yelling instead of talking, and we're the only ones who can fix that."

Cupcake stared up at Alec with unseeing glass eyes and a wise old philosophical smile.

"And you know what the worst part is?" Alec went on. He sniffed, tears starting to fill his eyes again. "Stevie never knew I loved him at all." A sharp pain constricted Alec's throat, and a sob escaped his lips. Then another and another. He curled up around the bear and lay back, sobbing until the worst of the pain ebbed away. Then he lay still for a long time, just thinking. At last he sat up.

Stevie was gone. There was nothing he could do about

that. It was a private pain that he would have to live with forever. But maybe there was something he could do about the rest of his family. He picked Cupcake up and carried him down to the family room. He sat down cross-legged next to Kelly and cleared his throat.

"I love you, Kelly," he said.

Kelly gave him a startled look. "What did you say?"

"I said, I love you."

Kelly screwed up her eyes and leaned away from him. "What, are you getting kinky now?" she asked.

Alec frowned. "Of course I'm not getting kinky. I'm your brother. I'm supposed to love you."

"Yeah, but you're not supposed to *say* it."

"Why not?"

"'Cause it's not cool, that's why."

Kelly got to her feet and picked up her sandwich plate. Alec got up, too, and followed her out to the kitchen.

"I don't care," he said. "I love you, and I want you to know it."

Kelly eyed him suspiciously. "Why?"

"Because I'm tired of the way things are in this family. I want it to be like it used to be when we were little, when we cared about each other and did things together."

Kelly ran her dish under the water. "Like what?"

"Like" — Alec thought for a minute — "like the gingerbread house. Remember the gingerbread house?"

Kelly shut off the water and turned slowly from the sink. "Yeah," she said softly. A smile played around her lips and she nodded. "Yeah, I remember."

"And stringing popcorn, and making decorations.

Look at this place. You'd never know Christmas Eve was three days away."

Kelly looked around the kitchen, and an expression of sadness darkened her eyes. "I know," she said, "but we're not little kids anymore."

"Stop saying that," said Alec. "What does that have to do with anything? We're still a family. We can still do things together." Suddenly he had an idea.

"Kelly," he said, "let's go buy a Christmas tree."

Kelly screwed up her eyes again. "We have a Christmas tree."

"Not that kind," said Alec. "The real kind, like we used to get. Remember?"

Kelly started to smile.

"Remember how we used to drive Dad nuts?" Alec went on. "We'd have to go to every lot in town —"

Kelly started to laugh. "Yeah, and then we'd make him buy one that was, like, ten feet tall, and it'd cost him a fortune."

Alec was laughing now, too. "And then he'd get it home and have to cut three feet off so it would fit in the living room —"

Kelly was doubled over, holding her sides. "And then the trunk was so thick it wouldn't fit into the stand!"

They both slid down on the floor and laughed until they were out of breath. Alec felt guilty laughing, but it felt so good. It had been so long.

Kelly rolled over on her back and lay there for a while, catching her breath. Then suddenly she sat up. "Let's do it!" she said.

CHAPTER 25

Kelly had convinced Alec that their mother would take a dim view of a real Christmas tree in her formal living room, so they had settled on the family room. They were trying to wrestle the Christmas tree into its stand when the garage door opened and their father walked in.

"What on earth is going on here?" he asked.

Alec and Kelly grinned at each other through the branches.

"We bought a Christmas tree," said Alec.

"But . . . we have a Christmas tree."

"Not this kind," said Kelly. "This kind smells great!"

Alec's father took a big sniff and raised an eyebrow. "Yeah," he said. "It does smell pretty good."

"Could you do us a favor, Dad?" asked Alec. "Could you get down under there and screw it into the stand?"

Alec's father gave him a skeptical glance, but then he tossed his racquetball racquet onto the couch and came over and got down on his knees. He crawled under the tree.

"This trunk is way too big!" he shouted.

Alec and Kelly giggled. "We, uh, had to cut a little bit off the tree," said Alec.

"Yeah," said Kelly. "We bought it just a scooch too big."

"A scooch?" said their father. "What's a scooch?"

Alec shrugged. "About three feet."

His father rolled out from under the tree and stared at him. "*This*," he said, "is exactly why we stopped buying live trees in the first place."

Alec shrugged apologetically, and his father rolled his eyes. Alec glanced at Kelly, and they burst out laughing. Their father held out for a few seconds, and then he burst out laughing, too.

"All right," he said. "I'll go get the saw."

Half an hour later the tree was finally in the stand. They stood back to look at it.

"Uh-oh," said Alec. It was standing at about a forty-five-degree angle.

Alec's father frowned. "Nice tree you guys picked out," he said. "Did anybody think to check the trunk?"

Alec bent down, pushed the branches aside, and peeked at the trunk. "It's bent," he said.

Kelly burst out laughing again.

Alec's father shook his head. "I don't believe this," he grumbled good-naturedly.

After another half hour, the stand was nailed to the

floor, a broom handle was wedged between the tree and the wall, and —

"Yay!" shouted Kelly. "It's straight!"

They all cheered.

"*What's all this?*"

Alec turned around. His mother was standing in the hall, briefcase in hand. "What's going on here?" she asked again.

"We're putting up the Christmas tree," Alec's father stated matter-of-factly.

"But . . . what happened to the old one?"

"Nothing happened to the old one. The kids just decided they wanted a good old-fashioned Christmas tree, that's all. Come on over and smell it."

Alec's mother still looked skeptical, but she dropped her briefcase on the couch and walked over and stuck her nose into the tree. There was a sudden loud crack, a shriek, the sound of breaking glass. . . . And then the Christmas tree was tilted at a forty-five-degree angle again — right through the middle of the picture window!

CHAPTER 26

Alec sat quietly in the backseat of the car on the way home from church Christmas Eve. Things hadn't worked out quite the way he'd hoped. Life wasn't like *Leave It to Beaver,* it seemed. Changing his family back wasn't going to be as easy as telling them all he loved them and putting up an old-fashioned Christmas tree. In fact, he was slowly coming to realize that there would be no going back. He had created this new family, and he would have to learn to live with them. They weren't the worst family in the world. They just weren't his.

The hardest part was missing Stevie. It was so hard to mourn someone when there was no one to share the grief with. Alec felt that he would never be carefree again. Never be at peace. Never live without painful memories. Yohilda had said that in time he would forget, but Alec didn't want to forget, ever. He would do everything he could to keep Stevie alive, if only in his heart. He stared up at the sky now, remembering how Stevie used to excitedly search it on Christmas Eve for a glowing red nose.

"Looking for Rudolph?" Alec's father teased. He smiled at Alec in the rearview mirror.

Alec smiled sadly in return. "Yeah."

At home Alec sat listening to the soft carols on the stereo and staring at the artificial Christmas tree. It would have looked warmer, he thought, with some of Stevie's dumb little homemade ornaments on it.

Alec's mother and father walked in with cups of hot chocolate. "You're sure you don't want any?" his mother asked.

Alec shook his head.

"You're awfully quiet tonight," Alec's father said. "Everything okay?"

Alec nodded, then looked away so they couldn't see the truth in his eyes.

"Christmas Eve is such a peaceful night, isn't it?" Alec's mother said.

"Mmmm." Alec's father nodded. They sat down together on the couch.

Alec stared at the fireplace, blazing merrily. Stevie never would have let them have a fire. He would have been afraid Santa might get burned.

"Can we put out cookies and milk?" Alec asked suddenly.

His mother smiled. "Well, sure, if you want to." She winked at him. "I wonder if they'll disappear overnight?"

Yeah, thought Alec ruefully. Maybe they will, and maybe Santa Claus will bring Stevie back.

The front doorbell rang.

"I'll get it," Kelly yelled from the kitchen.

Alec's mother looked at his father. "I wonder who that could be," she said.

"Oh, Al-ec," Kelly called in a teasing voice. "It's for you-ou."

Alec shrugged in answer to his parents' questioning glances, then got up and walked out into the kitchen. Kelly walked by and gave him a mysterious wink. To his surprise he found Abbey Bennett waiting for him in the front hall. She smiled when she saw him.

"Hi, Alec," she said.

"Uh, hi," Alec stammered, his face growing warm.

"How've you been?"

"Good," said Alec awkwardly. "How 'bout you?"

"Good," said Abbey brightly. "I brought you something."

"You did?"

"Yeah. It's the bill from the hospital."

Alec could feel his face blanching.

Abbey giggled. "I'm only teasing," she said, giving his arm a playful squeeze, "but I really did bring you something." She started rummaging in her pocketbook. "I found it in my purse today. I'd forgotten all about it. Yohilda gave it to me, that day at the mall when I offered her a ride." Abbey continued to dig around. "Oh, here it is." She drew something out and held it in her hand.

Alec's breath caught in his throat.

"She said something about a wish," Abbey went on, giving an amused little laugh. "I told you, I think she was a bit eccentric. But anyway, I know she meant a lot to you, and I thought you might like to have it, as a keepsake."

Alec still stared, afraid to breathe for fear that the talisman might disappear.

"Alec? Don't you want it? Alec, I wish —"

"*No!*" Alec yelled, grabbing the talisman from Abbey's hand. "I-I mean yes. Of course I want it." His heart was pounding. Abbey had almost wished away his last chance to get Stevie back.

Abbey was looking at him strangely. "Are you okay?" she asked. "You look a little pale."

Alec waited until his breathing returned to normal. "Yeah," he said. "I . . . I'm fine. I was just . . . so touched . . . that you would want to give it to me."

Abbey shrugged. "Well, I doubt it's worth anything," she said.

"It *is* to me," said Alec.

Abbey smiled again. "I hoped it would be." She stretched up on tiptoes and planted a kiss on his cheek. "Merry Christmas," she told him.

Alec blushed. "Thanks," he said, then added silently, You have no idea how merry you just made it.

Alec saw Abbey to the door and watched her until her car drove out of sight. He touched the cheek that she had kissed, then squeezed the talisman in his hand. A shock of joy surged through his body. He turned and bounded up the stairs two at a time. He pulled his bedroom door closed behind him and leaned back against it, catching his breath. He stared into the darkness.

Suddenly he was scared, really scared. What if it didn't work? What if it only worked for the person it was given to? What if he made a mistake? What if he said the wrong thing? This was his only chance. He couldn't afford to blow it.

Alec walked slowly over to his bed and lay down. He closed his eyes. His heart thumped, and the blood pounded in his ears. "God," he whispered, "please let this work. Please let me say the right thing." He squeezed the talisman tight in his hand.

"I wish . . . I wish that I had never made my first wish

CHAPTER 27

Alec slowly opened his eyes. His room was flooded with light. He looked down at his hand. The talisman was gone. He turned quickly and stared out the window. The world was covered with a thick blanket of new snow, and the sun was climbing in the east. It was morning.

There was a soft knock at the door. Alec turned and watched as the knob turned, the door swung open, and a little, tear-streaked face peeked in.

Stevie!

"My God," Alec whispered. "Stevie! Is it really you?" He bolted from his bed, tripped over the rug in his haste, and landed with a jolt on his knees.

"Alec?" Stevie ran into the room. "Are you okay?"

Alec grabbed Stevie and hugged him desperately, marveling at the sweaty smell of his hair, the solid, flesh-and-blood feel of his body, and the warm touch of his chubby cheek.

"Stevie, it *is* you," he murmured, stroking Stevie's hair. "You're really here."

Stevie pulled back and gave him a puzzled look.

"Let me look at you," said Alec. He pushed Stevie back at arm's length. "You look okay. How do you feel? Where have you been? Do you remember anything about it?"

Stevie scrunched up his eyes. "I been in the kitchen," he said.

"In the kitchen? All this time?"

"All what time? It just happened a little while ago."

It was Alec's turn to be confused. "What just happened?"

"The fight."

"What fight?"

"The one between you and me, and then I told Mom and Dad about you leaving me at the mall." Stevie lowered his eyes. "I came up to say I'm sorry," he mumbled. "I'm sorry I got you in trouble."

Alec sat back on his knees and looked around. He was in his underwear, and his quilt lay strewn across his rumpled bunk. His jeans lay in the middle of the floor where he'd kicked them the morning of the fight. He'd gone back then, in time. Back to that morning.

Or had he?

Alec shook his head and stared at Stevie. "What day is it?" he asked.

"Saturday."

"And we just went to the mall yesterday?"

Stevie nodded.

"And we just had that big fight a little while ago?"

Stevie nodded again, sheepishly.

Alec stared at his bed and his quilt and his open book. Could he have fallen asleep reading? Could it have been a dream after all?

Alec let out a long sigh. Of course it had. That explained everything.

"What's wrong?" asked Stevie.

Alec shook his head. "Nothing," he said. "I just had the weirdest dream of my life. It seemed so *real*."

"What was it about?" asked Stevie.

Alec looked at him and smiled. "You."

"Me?"

"Yeah."

"What about me?"

Alec smiled. "Nothing." He tousled Stevie's hair. "It's a long story. But I want you to know something. I want you to know that I love you."

Stevie's eyes widened. "You do?"

"Of course I do." Alec gave him a quick hug, then added affectionately, "You little butt head."

Stevie positively beamed. "I love you, too," he said shyly.

"Good," said Alec. "Now that we got that straight, let's go downstairs. I want to apologize to Mom and Dad."

A shadow of doubt darkened Stevie's expression. "Do you think that's a good idea?" he said. "They're pretty mad."

Alec nodded. "Yeah," he said. "I think it's a good idea." He picked up his jeans and started putting them on.

"What's this?" asked Stevie. He reached out and picked something up off the floor.

Alec's heart squeezed when he saw it. The talisman. He took a deep breath and forced his heart to relax. It was just a dream, he told himself. He took the coin from Stevie's hand and stared at it.

"Hey," said Stevie. "Give that back. It's a Fun World token."

"It is not," said Alec, "it's a —"

"It is, too!" shrieked Stevie, grabbing for the coin. "Give it to me. I saw it first. Mommy!"

Alec clapped a hand over Stevie's mouth and the old anger flared inside him for a moment. Then he took a deep breath and shook his head.

"Hey," he whispered, "don't you think you've already gotten me in enough trouble for one morning?"

The fury drained from Stevie's eyes and was replaced by a look of repentance. He nodded, and Alec took his hand away.

"Besides," said Alec, "it's *not* a Fun World token."

"Well, what is it then?" asked Stevie.

"It's a talisman."

"A what?"

"Just a trinket some old lady gave me." Alec held it up, then looked at Stevie and smiled mysteriously. "If you could have one wish," he asked, "what would you wish for?"

Stevie grinned. "That's easy," he said. "A million more wishes!"

Alec laughed. "Yeah." He nodded.

"Is that what *you'd* wish for, too?" asked Stevie, obviously eager to continue the game.

Alec rubbed the coin between his thumb and fingers as he stared down into Stevie's bright, adoring eyes. He thought about the old woman, probably out there somewhere, in the cold and the snow.

"No," he said quietly.

"Then what would you wish for?" asked Stevie.

Alec slowly closed his hand over the talisman and squeezed it tight. "I would just wish . . . ," he said softly, "that our world was a kinder place."

Stevie screwed up his eyes and wrinkled his nose. "That's a funny wish," he said.

Alec smiled and opened his hand again.

It was empty.